绝句汉译

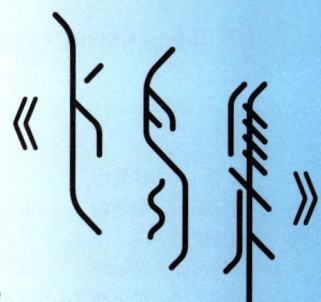

Stray Birds:
A Chinese Translation of
Cut Verses

程永生 译著

外语教学与研究出版社
FOREIGN LANGUAGE TEACHING AND RESEARCH PRESS
北京 BEIJING

图书在版编目（CIP）数据

绝句汉译《飞鸟集》：汉、英 / 程永生译著. -- 北京：外语教学与研究出版社，2020.12
ISBN 978-7-5213-2225-5

Ⅰ. ①绝… Ⅱ. ①程… Ⅲ. ①诗集－印度－现代－汉、英 Ⅳ. ①I351.25

中国版本图书馆 CIP 数据核字 (2020) 第 237855 号

出 版 人　徐建忠
责任编辑　李婉婧
责任校对　闫　璟
装帧设计　黄　浩
出版发行　外语教学与研究出版社
社　　址　北京市西三环北路 19 号（100089）
网　　址　http://www.fltrp.com
印　　刷　北京盛通印刷股份有限公司
开　　本　787×1092　1/32
印　　张　11.5
版　　次　2020 年 12 月第 1 版　2020 年 12 月第 1 次印刷
书　　号　ISBN 978-7-5213-2225-5
定　　价　53.90 元

购书咨询：(010) 88819926　电子邮箱：club@fltrp.com
外研书店：https://waiyants.tmall.com
凡印刷、装订质量问题，请联系我社印制部
联系电话：(010) 61207896　电子邮箱：zhijian@fltrp.com
凡侵权、盗版书籍线索，请联系我社法律事务部
举报电话：(010) 88817519　电子邮箱：banquan@fltrp.com
物料号：322250001

前言

　　泰戈尔1913年获得诺贝尔文学奖,是获此殊荣的第一位亚洲作家,也因之在我国闻名遐迩。有人曾将其获奖作品《吉檀迦利》译成汉语,其他诗作如《飞鸟集》也早有汉译,但所译多为散体。我最近几年开始诗词散曲写作,且日觉兴致盎然,似乎有用格律诗词看待整个世界之势。当我从网上看到《飞鸟集》时,怎么也挡不住将其译成格律诗的欲望,尽管我当时正忙于其他事。

　　选用什么样的格律诗翻译《飞鸟集》呢?《飞鸟集》共325首散体诗,多为一两个诗句,且意象丛集。译成格律诗,有三大难关:平仄、押韵和对仗。如译成律诗,对仗是不可逾越的。即使译成词或散曲,也经常会遇到对仗问题。不是说译诗不能对仗,而是因为律诗的颔联与颈联一般必须对仗。词和散曲,哪些对仗哪些不对仗,哪些诗句对仗,哪些诗句不对仗,多有严格的规定。只有绝句比较自由,可以一联对仗另一联不对仗,可以两联都对仗,还可以两联都不对仗。再说,绝句的平仄和押韵的规律性很强,比较好把握。

中国是诗词散曲之国,近现代虽一度几起几落,但最近几年,随着改革开放的深入进展,更是高潮迭起。遍布社区的老年大学都有诗词班,差不多每个单位都有诗词学会,诗词微信群远多于其他微信群,诗词报刊也应运而生,为什么还要多此一举,将外国的散体诗译成绝句呢?

问题的答案就在于"外国"二字,须知泰戈尔的《飞鸟集》从内容到形式都有别于中国的格律诗词。例如,诗集一开始便将离群临窗的夏鸟与秋天的叶、将鸟的歌声与落叶的飘零、将鸟的告别与叶子落地的哀叹置于一处,相互参照,使人浮想联翩。第二首,诗人请一群漂泊世界的小流浪汉,将自己的足印留在诗人的诗句之中。这难道不是说,诗人是要用自己的诗句踏遍全球吗?第三首说,世界见到了自己的爱人,摘下了宽广无垠的面罩,便变小了,小成了一首歌,小成了一次永恒的吻。第四首说,是大地的眼泪使她的微笑鲜花盛开。第五首说威力无穷的沙漠,燃烧着去追寻小草的爱,小草则摇摇头,笑了笑,飞奔而去。

够了,所有这些在汉语的格律诗中,怎么都见不到。我们只有"众鸟高飞尽，孤云独去闲。相见两不厌，只有敬亭山"，"死去元知万事空，但悲不见九州同。王师北定中原日，家祭无忘告乃翁"。自唐宋以降，格律诗如何另辟蹊径，恐怕一直是诗人们苦思难解的问题。我自己觉得，读了泰戈尔的《飞鸟集》之后，思路开阔多了。如果这本《绝句汉译〈飞鸟集〉》面市之后，能为汉语绝句甚至诗词曲赋注入些许新鲜血液，我这几个月的汗就没有白流。诚如此，吾之幸也，岂有他哉？

　　本书翻译之际，我正在吉利学院任英语教授，得到了学院和人文分院的支持和鼓励，特向他们表示衷心的感谢。外语教学与研究出版社高英分社高度重视小书的出版，付出了辛勤劳动，特向他们表示衷心的感谢！

程永生
2020年7月15日

1

一

Stray birds of summer come to my window to sing and fly away.
And yellow leaves of autumn, which have no songs, flutter and fall there with a sigh.

几只夏天的流浪鸟,飞到我的窗前,欢唱了一气,又飞走了。
秋天的黄叶,没有歌声,飘飘荡荡,落在那儿,发出了一声叹息。

别群

夏鸟出群飞,临窗沐日晖。
欢歌三两遍,小别几时归?

秋叶

秋叶已枯黄,欢歌早早忘。
随风几起伏,着地叹凄凉。

夏鸟与黄叶

离群夏鸟几临窗,欢唱声声告别腔。
秋叶无歌飘荡荡,长吁短叹落何邦?

2

—

O troupe of little vagrants of the world, leave your footprints in my words.

哦,漂泊世界的团队,可爱的小流浪者们,请在我的诗中留下你们的脚印。

少年游

结队小儿孙,遨游世界村。
萍踪生浪迹,尽在我诗存。

3

—

The world puts off its mask of vastness to its lover.
It becomes small as one song, as one kiss of the eternal.

面对心爱的人,世界摘下了他宽广无边的面具。
他变小了,小成一支歌,小成一次永恒的吻。

世界旷无涯

世界旷无涯,亲来去面纱。
缩身成永吻,又似小歌芽。

4

一

It is the tears of the earth that keep her smiles in bloom.

是大地的泪花,使她的微笑变成了常开不谢的花。

大地轻垂泪

大地轻垂泪,群山尽着花。
红黄争俊俏,微笑接天涯。

5

一

The mighty desert is burning for the love of a blade of grass who shakes her head and laughs and flies away.

无垠的沙漠,燃烧着炙热去追寻一叶小草的爱,可小草摇了摇头,笑了笑,便飞走了。

旷漠大无垠

旷漠大无垠,勤追绿草唇。
摇头忙拒绝,飞笑别高邻。

6

—

If you shed tears when you miss the sun, you also miss the stars.

1）如果失去太阳就潸然泪下，你也会失去星星的。
2）如果想念太阳就潸然泪下，你也会想念星星的。

羲和与群星

羲和出海送温馨,汝失金乌泪怎停?
浓意浓情浓几许,伤心掩面哭群星。

何时二者能相会

思念骄阳热泪潸,日光普照众星闲。
何时二者能相会,免却柔肠昼夜弯。

---

* 原文miss一语双关,汉语没找到对应词,故分译之。

7

—

The sands in your way beg for your song and your movement, dancing water. Will you carry the burden of their lameness?

流水舞从容,泥沙沿途乞你的歌声、乞你奔腾。君愿负重前行,裹挟瘸腿的泥沙奔流吗?

泥沙俱下

流水滔滔舞纵横,河沙半道乞歌声。
愿君善举施无歇,挟裹瘸泥大海行。

8

———

Her wishful face haunts my dreams like the rain at night.

睡梦沉沉,她那期盼的脸庞,时隐时现,就像夜雨淅沥一般。

热脸递需求

热脸递需求,诚如夜雨流。
来回温旧梦,潮涌乱心舟。

9

—

Once we dreamt that we were strangers.
We wake up to find that we were dear to each other.

他日睡梦之中,你我形同陌路。
醒来却看到,彼此都挺亲近。

似曾相识

他夜睡朦胧,人人似未逢。
醒来方忆起,彼此爱融融。

10

Sorrow is hushed into peace in my heart like the evening among the silent trees.

忧愁一入胸怀就悄无声息了,就像夜晚混迹于恬静的森林一般。

心壑好埋愁

心壑好埋愁,神安岂有忧。
夜潜林寂寞,何处觅从头。

11

—

Some unseen fingers, like an idle breeze, are playing upon my heart the music of the ripples.

有些看不见的手指,就像闲散的微风一样,在我的心上,弹拨着涟漪的音乐。

神奇手指视无形

神奇手指视无形,慢拂徐飞岂有停。
骤拨琴弦三五曲,涟漪美乐搅心宁。

12

" What language is thine, O sea?"
"The language of eternal question."
"What language is thy answer, O sky?"
"The language of eternal silence."

"哦,大海,你使用什么语言?"
"无休止的疑问。"
"哦,蓝天,你使用什么语言来回答?"
"无休止的沉默。"

疑问与沉默

海水用何言,追根诘问繁。
蓝天呈答语,沉默少愁烦。

13

—

Listen, my heart, to the whispers of the world with which it makes love to you.

听吧,我的心。听世界微语绵绵,叙说着对你的爱。

吾心静静听

吾心静静听,世界唤无停。
款语揉浓意,微风送爱馨。

14

The mystery of creation is like the darkness of night—it is great. Delusions of knowledge are like the fog of the morning.

创造的神秘,就像漆黑的夜晚那样,它是伟大的。知识的魔幻,有如晨雾。

创造与知识

创造秘微微,诚如夜幕徽。
新知多梦幻,酷似雾晨飞。

15

Do not seat your love upon a precipice because it is high.

不要将你的爱挂在悬崖峭壁上,那儿太高了。

峭壁与情爱

巍峨峭壁高,情爱怎拴牢。
一旦悬空半,终生伴草蒿。

16

I sit at my window this morning where the world like a passer-by stops for a moment, nods to me and goes.

今晨我坐在窗前,看到世界有如匆匆过客,打那儿路过,停了片刻,朝我点了点头就走了。

过客人世

晨起坐窗前,红尘走陌阡。
憩休方片刻,道别又扬鞭。

17

—

These little thoughts are the rustle of leaves; they have their whisper of joy in my mind.

那些些微的想法,都是些沙沙的落叶,在我的心头高兴得喃喃细语。

思绪与私语

思绪特精微,沙沙落叶飞。
欢愉私窃语,排闼在心扉。

18

―

What you are you do not see, what you see is your shadow.

你看不见自己是什么样的,你能见到的,只是自己的影子。

自审自身难

自审自身难,徘徊见影残。
请君斟酌细,勤顾保平安。

19

My wishes are fools, they shout across thy song, my Master.
Let me but listen.

我的希望,尽是些傻乎乎的东西。主啊,它们呼喊着穿越您的歌声。那就让我听着吧。

希望与圣曲

希望多愚蠢,喧嚣圣曲中。
问君何以对,恭听待其终。

20

I cannot choose the best.
The best chooses me.

我无法选择最佳。
最佳却选中了我。

鳌头自有舟

寻佳逐一流,愚陋实难求。
水到渠成日,鳌头自有舟。

21

———

They throw their shadows before them who carry their lantern on their back.

那些将灯背在背上的人,将自己的影子投到了身前。

背灯投影

明灯扛背上,投影到身前。
左右相交替,腾挪讲后先。

22

—

That I exist is a perpetual surprise which is life.

我的存在永远让我惊叹不已,这就是生活。

心扉顿洞开

缘何吾命在,神秘永难猜。
生活诚如此,心扉顿洞开。

23

—

"We, the rustling leaves, have a voice that answers the storms,
 but who are you so silent?"
"I am a mere flower."

"我们都是些沙沙的落叶,用声音来回答暴风雨。可你是谁呀,却这般悄无声息?"
"我仅仅是一朵花。"

我乃一朵花

落叶沙沙回暴雨,君何寂寞又沉沦?
乡邻见问慌忙答,我仅凡花倩女身。

24

Rest belongs to the work as the eyelids to the eyes.

休息服从于工作,就像眼睑服从于眼睛一样。

作息

作息当如何?双双各几多?
诸君康眼睑,阿睹有人呵。

25

—

Man is a born child, his power is the power of growth.

人一生下来是个孩子,其力量来源于成长。

成长与力量

初生力几何?渐长渐增多。
岁月资强壮,年轮疗病疴。

26

God expects answers for the flowers he sends us, not for the sun and the earth.

上帝希望我们呵护他送给我们的花,而不是太阳和土地。

护花

上帝赠鲜花,望我呵护她。
阳光不用管,大地自有家。

关心

鲜花天帝赠,诚望子关心。
大地何须护?朝阳孰敢侵?

27

—

The light that plays, like a naked child, among the green leaves happily knows not that man can lie.

光,像一个裸体小孩一样,在绿叶中尽情地耍戏,全然不知人还会撒谎。

无知几许呆

光如裸体孩,耍叶乐悠哉。
尘世多欺诈,无知几许呆。

28

―

O Beauty, find thyself in love, not in the flattery of thy mirror.

啊,美人,请在爱中而不要在镜子的奉承中寻找自我吧。

切莫咨明镜

诚心语美人,挚爱可容身。
切莫咨明镜,阿谀会失真。

阿谀且失真

我欲语美人,爱中有自身。
切莫信明镜,阿谀且失真。

29

My heart beats her waves at the shore of the world and writes upon it her signature in tears with the words, "I love thee."

我的心在世界的岸边涌起波涛,在上面用泪水书写出她的签名,说:"我爱你。"

一行一爱一姗姗

心潮涌浪浪侵滩,热泪题签几日干?
浓墨浓情浓笔底,一行一爱一姗姗。

30

―

"Moon, for what do you wait?"
"To salute the sun for whom I must make way."

"月亮呀,你在等什么呢?"
"等着向太阳致敬,我必须给他让位。"

让贤

朗月缘何未易弦?彼言让位与高贤。
朝晖一抹山河醉,公子王孙敬浩天。

31

———

The trees come up to my window like the yearning voice of the dumb earth.

那些树就像哑巴了的大地带着渴求的呼喊,来到了我的窗前。

怎表愿千千

绿树到窗前,声如哑地弦。
吐心音不济,怎表愿千千。

32

His own mornings are new surprises to God.

上帝对自己的每个清晨都感到新奇。

清晨日日鲜

清晨日日鲜,愈变愈婵娟。
上帝诚知晓,惊奇每一天。

神奇逐日新

上帝享清晨,神奇逐日新。
天天惊喜悦,运转赖冬春。

33

—

Life finds its wealth by the claims of the world, and its worth by the claims of love.

生命声称拥有世界而富甲天下,声称拥有大爱而身价超群。

生命富有自何来

生命富有自何来?声称拥有全世界。
生命价值自何来?声称拥有绵绵爱。

大千世界怎言多

生命资财费琢磨,大千世界怎言多?
胸怀厚爱连城价,小惠微恩值几何?

34

The dry river-bed finds no thanks for its past.

干涸的河床对既往不知感恩。

床不谢恩波

烈日烤溪河，干沙露几多。
也曾清水漫，床不谢恩波。

35

一

The bird wishes it were a cloud.
The cloud wishes it were a bird.

那只鸟说,它要是一朵云就好了。
那朵云说,它要是一只鸟就好了。

云和鸟

云飞鸟亦飞,各自展芳菲。
鸟羡游云浪,云奇众鸟威。

36

—

The waterfall sings, "I find my song, when I find my freedom."

瀑布唱着说:"只要有自由,我就想放声歌唱。"

瀑布歌自由

条条瀑布挂山前,日夜欢腾走大川。
演唱为何难止息,自由启闸响歌弦。

37

—

I cannot tell why this heart languishes in silence.
It is for small needs it never asks, or knows or remembers.

我真不知道,这颗心为何悄然憔悴。
为那些从不需要、从不知晓、从不记忆的小东小西。

吾心乏语时

吾心乏语时,憔悴有谁知。
小事常牵挂,愁烦自惹之。

38

―

Woman, when you move about in your household service your limbs sing like a hill stream among its pebbles.

妇人,当你干家务的时候跑来跑去,四肢在歌唱,就像山边的溪流在鹅卵石之间穿流一样。

欢歌舞四肢

妇女理家时,欢歌舞四肢。
宛如溪涧水,抚石笑嘻嘻。

39

—

The sun goes to cross the Western sea, leaving its last salutation to the East.

太阳将穿越西边的大海,最后深情地向东方辞别。

怎舍依依别

斜阳越海西,回首向东稽。
怎舍依依别,情深泪眼凄。

40

―

Do not blame your food because you have no appetite.

没有胃口时,请不要拿美食出气。

不吃一何痴

珍馐满桌时,不吃一何痴。
休怨佳肴少,皆缘乏味滋。

41

—

The trees, like the longings of the earth, stand a-tiptoe to peep at the heaven.

那些树,像渴望的大地一样,踮起脚尖,窥视天堂。

昂头踮脚一何痴

细看大地瞭空时,热切心情孰悉知?
诸树好奇思睥睨,昂头踮脚一何痴。

42

—

You smiled and talked to me of nothing and I felt that for this I had been waiting long.

你微笑着对我说话,毫无内容,可我却感到,对此,我已经等待很久了。

空谷足音

朗笑微嘻岂有心,儒谈雅吐乏浑金。
多情久盼君唇启,空谷欣闻尔足音。

43

—

The fish in the water is silent, the animal on the earth is noisy,
 the bird in the air is singing.
But Man has in him the silence of the sea, the noise of the earth
 and the music of the air.

鱼在水里悄无声息,动物在地球上吵吵嚷嚷,鸟儿在天空中歌声嘹亮。
人如大海,悄无声息;人如大地,吵吵嚷嚷;人如天空,歌声嘹亮。

吾人静闹任纵横

游鱼戏水悄无声,走兽驰山吼叫盈。
飞鸟行空歌不歇,吾人静闹任纵横。

44

—

The world rushes on over the strings of the lingering heart making the music of sadness.

缠绵的心弦弹出了悲伤的乐章,世界跨过它匆匆向前。

缠绵纠结恼心弦

缠绵纠结恼心弦,弹拨忧伤四五篇。
世界驱驰难止息,乐章横跨一无牵。

45

一

He has made his weapons his gods.
When his weapons win he is defeated himself.

他把刀枪视为神灵。
而刀枪显威之日,却是自败之时。

唱罢哀歌唱自殇

箭弩稀珍似上苍,强朋弱党试锋芒。
何愁浊世无人敌,唱罢哀歌唱自殇。

46

God finds himself by creating.

上帝在创造中找到了自我。

创造之中有自身

伊甸经营几苦辛,凡尘懵懂怎知因。
人言顿悟千疑解,创造之中有自身。

47

———

Shadow, with her veil drawn, follows Light in secret meekness, with her silent steps of love.

阴影戴上了面纱,秘密地、温驯地、悄悄地踏着爱的节拍,跟在光的身后。

躬身秘密逐光华

暗影阴阴罩面纱,躬身秘密逐光华。
息声踏拍皆缘爱,上下高低缓缓爬。

48

The stars are not afraid to appear like fireflies.

即使看上去像萤火虫,那些星星也毫无惧色。

小虫萤火亦飞虹

群星闪闪亮晴空,正视斜观各不同。
远近高低随意变,小虫萤火亦飞虹。

49

—

I thank thee that I am none of the wheels of power but I am one with the living creatures that are crushed by it.

谢谢你,我没有成为权势的一个车轮,却成了被碾压的芸芸众生中的一员。

碾压非吾愿

躬身谢主神,权势铸车轮。
碾压非吾愿,同侪垫底人。

50

The mind, sharp but not broad, sticks at every point but does not move.

心灵尖尖却不宽厚,每一个尖端都在探头探脑,但却按兵不动。

心灵锐锐竿

心灵锐锐竿,尖刻却无宽。
探脑时时易,陈兵处处难。

51

—

Your idol is shattered in the dust to prove that God's dust is greater than your idol.

你的偶像在粉尘中跌得粉粹,足以证明,上帝的粉尘比你的偶像还要伟大。

先生崇偶像

先生崇偶像,偶像毁尘埃,
上帝尘埃伟,君为偶像哀。

上苍亘古雄威巨

偶像崇高坐拜台,红尘跌落瞬时栽。
上苍亘古雄威巨,强弱高低岂用猜?

52

Man does not reveal himself in his history, he struggles up through it.

人在自己的历史中难以崭露头角,却搏杀着穿越历史。

缓缓熬煎缓缓诗

历史长流北斗移,吾侪展露恐难之。
匆匆搏杀匆匆客,缓缓熬煎缓缓诗。

53

—

While the glass lamp rebukes the earthen for calling it cousin, the moon rises, and the glass lamp, with a bland smile, calls her, —"My dear, dear sister."

玻璃灯责怪陶土灯称自己为堂弟。月亮升起来了,玻璃灯却旁若无人地微笑着喊道:"我亲爱的,亲爱的姐姐。"

玻璃陶瓷两明灯

玻璃陶瓷两明灯,前者责其以表凌。
适逢明月生天际,微笑亲姐叫几声。

玻璃灯与陶瓷灯

不同质地两明灯,玻责陶瓷以表凌。
为显位尊求朗月,淡呼亲姐殷呼肱。

54

Like the meeting of the seagulls and the waves we meet and come near. The seagulls fly off, the waves roll away and we depart.

就像海鸥和海浪一样,我们相聚了,我们靠近了。海鸥飞离了,海浪滚滚向前,我们也话别了。

相遇相离浪与鸥

相遇相离浪与鸥,几分几聚几回眸。
舔波冲浪鸥飞去,一往无前浪岂留。

55

一

My day is done, and I am like a boat drawn on the beach,
 listening to the dance-music of the tide in the evening.

我的白天已经完了,现在像一只小船搁浅在海滩,入夜静听海潮起舞的音乐。

起落狂潮几亮喉

人老时衰日尽头,一如搁浅海滩舟。
夜听巨浪翩翩舞,起落狂潮几亮喉。

56

―

Life is given to us, we earn it by giving it.

生命已经赋予我们了,只有充实生活才能活得津津有味。

一趟红尘一趟诗

天赋人生孰不知,充盈尚赖自为之。
若能善用光阴尺,一趟红尘一趟诗。

57

—

We come nearest to the great when we are great in humility.

当我们成了谦卑中的伟人时,便最接近伟大。

伟大赖谦卑

伟大赖谦卑,吾侪勉力追。
菩提悬硕果,心手两相随。

不到功成志不移

人言伟大赖谦卑,不到功成志不移。
苦练勤思晨复夜,计程何日抵峨眉。

58

The sparrow is sorry for the peacock at the burden of its tail.

孔雀拖着长尾巴,麻雀却怕它负担过重而感到遗憾。

忧天麻雀鸟

孔雀尾巴长,开屏费力张。
忧天麻雀鸟,唯恐彼身伤。

麻雀追随孔雀飞

麻雀追随孔雀飞,忧其尾重虑其肥。
屏生五彩屏迷眼,开合轻松易发挥。

59

—

Never be afraid of the moments—thus sings the voice of the everlasting.

决不要怕那些时刻,永恒如此唱道。

桑田浪海任纵横

永恒喜爱唱声声,夏去秋来请勿惊。
万变循宗宗亦变,桑田浪海任纵横。

60

—

The hurricane seeks the shortest road by the no-road, and suddenly ends its search in the Nowhere.

飓风以弃道而行的方式寻找最近之道,又在乌有乡停止了搜索。

飓风寻道

欲抄近道走飓风,近道全在无道中。
霎时风平浪止息,搜寻止于虚无丛。

努力千番顷刻终

一路搜寻走飓风,欲抄近道道朦胧。
眼看已到虚无国,努力千番顷刻终。

61

―

Take my wine in my own cup, friend.
It loses its wreath of foam when poured into that of others.

朋友,请就我的杯喝我的酒吧。
要是倒到别人的杯子里,一圈酒沫就荡然无存了。

请就我杯饮

酒在我杯中,请就我杯饮。
若换他人杯,酒沫一无存。

君若换觥然后饮

葡萄美酒我杯中,务请先生酌此盅。
君若换觥然后饮,一圈泡沫失匆匆。

62

The Perfect decks itself in beauty for the love of the Imperfect.

完美把自己打扮得漂漂亮亮以追求不完美的爱。

取长补短可成春

完全欲吻不全唇,对镜梳妆扮一新。
过往行人询所以,取长补短可成春。

63

—

God says to man, "I heal you therefore I hurt, love you therefore punish."

神对人说:"伤害是为了治愈,惩罚是因为爱。"

情深深责罚

上帝语凡民,伤君在治身。
情深深责罚,大爱一何真。

64

―

Thank the flame for its light, but do not forget the lampholder standing in the shade with constancy of patience.

谢谢灯火带来了光明。但不要忘了那位掌灯人,他耐心地站在灯影下面初心不改。

掌灯人

烛焰赐光明,纷纷谢厚情。
勿忘阴影下,伫立掌灯生。

65

—

Tiny grass, your steps are small, but you possess the earth under your tread.

小小的草儿啊,你们的脚是那么的小,但却拥有脚下的大地。

小脚踩大地

声声呼小草,草小脚也小。
小脚踩大地,寰宇入怀抱。

怀抱寰球脑顶星

大地茫茫细草青,双双小脚瘦伶仃。
乍看总叹卑微贱,怀抱寰球脑顶星。

66

The infant flower opens its bud and cries, "Dear World, please do not fade."

稚嫩的花张开花蕾喊道:"亲爱的世界,可千万不要褪色啊。"

褪色乱花魂

花嫩一何纯,张蕾乞乾坤。
乞君休褪色,褪色乱花魂。

垂老焉能上雅台

稚嫩花芽蕾未开,欲求世界为何来?
乞君永葆青春色,垂老焉能上雅台。

67

—

God grows weary of great kingdoms, but never of little flowers.

上帝对那些庞大王国变得厌烦了,却从不厌烦那些小花。

大国与小花

大国特傲慢,上帝颇厌烦。
小花特谦恭,上帝颇喜欢。

鄙视强权袒弱妆

大国泱泱傲上苍,小花腼腆面颜藏。
九霄云外公心在,鄙视强权袒弱妆。

68

Wrong cannot afford defeat but Right can.

错误经不住失败,正确却不在乎。

错误与正确

错误本脆弱,难经失败磨。
正确颇雄伟,失败难攻破。

错误与正确

错误性情愚,难经失败诛。
此时看正确,惧色几全无。

错误与正确

错误初逢正确时,高低上下有谁知。
面临失败真形现,前者遭殃后者祺。

69

"I give my whole water in joy," sings the waterfall, "though little of it is enough for the thirsty."

瀑布唱道:"我兴高采烈地把所有的水都倒出来了,虽然稍有一点就是可解渴了。"

欢歌瀑布走岩巅

欢歌瀑布走岩巅,尽出涓涓峭壁悬。
一点诚然能解渴,竭囊可望凿深渊。

70

Where is the fountain that throws up these flowers in a ceaseless outbreak of ecstasy?

喷泉在哪儿？它那股不间断的狂喜，将那些水花喷得多高。

何地觅喷泉

何地觅喷泉？山边或路边。
水花狂发喜，雨雾射青天。

71

一

The woodcutter's axe begged for its handle from the tree.
The tree gave it.

樵夫的斧头找那棵树要个手柄。
树就给它了。

无柄正烦愁

樵夫有斧头,无柄正烦愁。
何不求诸树,枝条解困忧。

72

In my solitude of heart I feel the sigh of this widowed evening veiled with mist and rain.

内心很孤寂之际,我会感到,失偶的夜晚,笼罩在雾和雨之中,发出了叹息。

余心几独孤

余心几独孤,傍晚叹何愚。
雨雾交加际,唏嘘失偶无?

73

—

Chastity is a wealth that comes from abundance of love.

贞洁是财富,来源于丰裕的爱情。

贞洁铸资财

贞洁铸资财,全从厚爱来。
温情浓与淡,日夜适时栽。

74

—

The mist, like love, plays upon the heart of the hills and brings out surprises of beauty.

雾像爱情一样,在山峦的心尖上嬉戏,戏出了许多意想不到的美。

藏情密雾好调情

藏情密雾好调情,戏耍山心戏耍莺。
无意花开无意闹,一峰春色一峰萌。

75

—

We read the world wrong and say that it deceives us.

我们误读了世界,反说它在欺蒙我们。

寰球误读数吾侪

寰球误读数吾侪,不谢浓恩乱出牌。
生死枯荣谁做主,污之蒙骗失和谐。

76

The poet wind is out over the sea and the forest to seek his own voice.

诗人的风刮出来了,刮过了大海,刮过了森林,去寻找自己的声音。

猛刮诗家一阵风

猛刮诗家一阵风,漂洋过海树林中。
千端万件均无意,自己扬声自兴隆。

诗声盼自隆

骚人刮阵风,过海入林中。
君若询缘故,诗声盼自隆。

77

Every child comes with the message that God is not yet discouraged of man.

每个孩子都带来了这样的信息,上帝对人类没有灰心丧气。

上帝志无移

孩子出生时,传言父母知。
尔曹虽夯劣,上帝志无移。

78

The grass seeks her crowd in the earth.
The tree seeks his solitude of the sky.

那棵草在大地中寻找朋侣。
那棵树从天空中寻求独处。

绿草与大树

绿草觅朋邻，搜寻大地身。
高空求独处，巨树志何真。

79

—

Man barricades against himself.

人类阻塞了自己的前程。

群谋富万村

吾侪求发展,自堵自家门。
脱险凭何策,群谋富万村。

80

—

Your voice, my friend, wanders in my heart, like the muffled sound of the sea among these listening pines.

朋友,你的声音在我的心里回荡,就像在被压抑的海涛声在聆听海浪的松树丛中回荡一样。

君音荡我心

君音荡我心,闷抑海波吟。
袅袅穿林过,青松听浪侵。

81

—

What is this unseen flame of darkness whose sparks are the stars?

这看不见的漆黑的火焰,它的火花都是星星,它是什么呢?

黑夜卧纵横

黑夜卧纵横,明光看不清。
火花何物赐?星斗满天生。

82

Let life be beautiful like summer flowers and death like autumn leaves.

让生命像夏天的花朵一样美丽动人,让死亡像秋天的落叶一样枯槁。

花开生命旺

夏日百花浓,秋来百叶松。
花开生命旺,叶落总归宗。

83

He who wants to do good knocks at the gate; he who loves finds the gate open.

为了做好事的人敲门而进,为了爱的人却发现门是开着的。

心扉敞爱村

行好得敲门,心扉敞爱村。
相形无上下,明月慰诗魂。

84

In death the many becomes one; in life the one becomes many.
Religion will be one when God is dead.

死了,千命归一;活着,一命成千。
上帝一死,就千教合一了。

在世千般别

在世千般别,死后一宗归。
众教分流派,神死皆成灰。

人生在世别千千

人生在世别千千,死后相邀入土泉。
三教九流难尽数,神眠统统逐神眠。

85

The artist is the lover of Nature, therefore he is her slave and her master.

艺术家钟情于自然,既是自然的奴隶,也是自然的主人。

泼墨挥毫写九川

艺术钟情大自然,亦为奴隶亦为天。
须臾鬼使神差到,泼墨挥毫写九川。

86

"How far are you from me, O Fruit?"
"I am hidden in your heart, O Flower."

"啊,果儿。你离我有多远?"
"啊,花儿。我藏在你的心中。"

鲜花与水果

鲜花问果离多远,答曰潜藏朵里边。
一旦春容憔悴损,探头钻出尔心田。

87

This longing is for the one who is felt in the dark, but not seen in the day.

思念那夜晚感觉得到白天却看不见的人。

神思逐日飞

神思逐日飞,君问飞向谁?
黑夜能感知,白天倩影微。

思念无端四下飞

思念无端四下飞,恋花恋草恋蔷薇。
夜临西海姗姗会,日出东山速速归。

88

"You are the big drop of dew under the lotus leaf, I am the smaller one on its upper side," said the dewdrop to the lake.

露珠对湖水说:"你是荷叶下的大露珠,我是荷叶上面的小露珠。"

露珠湖水血缘亲

露珠湖水血缘亲,荷叶居中隔两珍。
大小诚然天壤别,悬殊上下总为邻。

89

The scabbard is content to be dull when it protects the keenness of the sword.

保护锋利的钢刀时,刀鞘乐于呆钝。

钝鞘建奇功

刃利剑生风,深藏厚革中。
锋芒从不露,钝鞘建奇功。

刀闪寒光刀不露

钢锋霍霍现锋芒,厚钝皮鞘彼可藏。
刀闪寒光刀不露,人持利刃免遭殃。

90

—

In darkness the One appears as uniform; in the light the One appears as manifold.

黑暗中,一看上去整齐划一;在光线下,一看上去千姿百态。

阳光映射万千重

横看成岭侧成峰,远近高低易面容。
一在暗中齐整整,阳光映射万千重。

91

—

The great earth makes herself hospitable with the help of the grass.

在绿草的帮助下,大地也变得殷勤好客了。

互助两峥嵘

小草绿莹莹,诚心玉地成。
殷勤招访客,互助两峥嵘。

92

—

The birth and death of the leaves are the rapid whirls of the eddy whose wider circles move slowly among stars.

死叶和生叶都成了涡流的旋转圈，圈小些的快速转动，圈大些的在星星当中缓慢地旋转。

叶生叶死旋涡流

叶生叶死旋涡流，疾快徐迟似荡舟。
圈小匝多加速转，绕星圆大慢悠悠。

93

—

Power said to the world, "You are mine."
The world kept it prisoner on her throne.
Love said to the world, "I am thine."
The world gave it the freedom of her house.

权势对世界说:"你属于我。"
世界却将权势变成了自己宝座上的囚徒。
爱情对世界说:"我属于你。"
世界却让她在自己的室内自由驰骋。

世界缘何围势权

世界缘何围势权？豪言少礼藐苍天。
心雄助长乾坤欲，身陷牢笼叹惘然。

爱恋缘何享自由

爱恋缘何享自由？愿随世界度春秋。
乾坤四壁乾坤小，浪漫晨昏浪漫舟。

权势·爱恋·世界

权势汹汹爱恋柔，面临世界比谋筹。
心骄气傲囚高阁，款语绵绵赐屋收。

94

一

The mist is like the earth's desire.
It hides the sun for whom she cries.

浓雾似乎了解大地的心愿,
它将大地呼之欲出的太阳藏起来了。

密雾浓云懂地球

密雾浓云懂地球,晨曦欲出顿时收。
若容烈日抛头面,万物枯焦万亩秋。

95

Be still, my heart, these great trees are prayers.

请安静点,我的心,那些参天大树正在祈祷呢。

吁请吾心休躁动

吁请吾心休躁动,参天大树铸森林。
缘何昼夜沙沙响,祈祷神歌诵到今。

96

The noise of the moment scoffs at the music of the Eternal.

瞬时的噪音嘲弄着永恒的音乐。

永恒美乐奏翩跹

永恒美乐奏翩跹,瞬刻心烦拨噪弦。
红眼安无红眼策,冷嘲热讽旷无前。

97

I think of other ages that floated upon the stream of life and love and death and are forgotten, and I feel the freedom of passing away.

我在浮想即逝的岁月,曾在生命、爱情和死亡的小溪上漂流,现在却被人遗忘了。我感触到了那无拘无束的匆匆过往。

亘古遥遥孰记全

亘古遥遥孰记全,爱情生死走浮川。
匆匆表演匆匆逝,闪闪风流闪闪烟。

98

一

The sadness of my soul is her bride's veil.
It waits to be lifted in the night.

我灵魂中的忧伤,是其新娘的盖头。
等到晚上将其揭开。

新娘渐展眉

灵魂几许悲,颇似盖头垂。
夜幕徐徐降,新娘渐展眉。

灵魂悲寂似婚纱

灵魂悲寂似婚纱,落泪伤心总有涯。
夜静更深红烛暖,盖头悄揭吻鲜花。

99

Death's stamp gives value to the coin of life; making it possible to buy with life what is truly precious.

死的钢印给生命的硬币标上了价值,于是便可以用生命来购买真正有价值的东西了。

换来无价或倾城

死亡钢印印人生,赋值高低业已明。
硬币随身能贸易,换来无价或倾城。

100

—

The cloud stood humbly in a corner of the sky.
The morning crowned it with splendour.

云彩卑躬地站在蓝天的一角,
晨曦使之异彩纷呈。

色彩缤纷虎豹纹

怯怯羞羞一朵云,天庭伫立侍贤君。
晨曦恻隐袭裳赠,色彩缤纷虎豹纹。

101

The dust receives insult and in return offers her flowers.

尘土遭到了作践却报之以鲜花。

大小恩仇一并歼

尘土蒙羞怨不添，鲜花数万释前嫌。
胸怀广阔无垠地，大小恩仇一并歼。

102

—

Do not linger to gather flowers to keep them, but walk on, for flowers will keep themselves blooming all your way.

不要踟蹰不前,收集鲜花,保存鲜花。径直朝前走吧,花会一路盛开的。

请勿踟蹰步不前

请勿踟蹰步不前,踏春采撷百花田。
劝君昂首休回首,万紫千红一路鲜。

103

Roots are the branches down in the earth.
Branches are roots in the air.

根是埋在地下的枝条,
枝条是伸在天空中的根。

几人悟透树根枝

松柏垂杨举世知,几人悟透树根枝?
自家兄弟原无异,入地升空两别离。

104

—

The music of the far-away summer flutters around the Autumn seeking its former nest.

夏天远去的音乐,围绕着秋天飘荡,以寻找昔日的栖息之巢。

袅袅余音几绕秋

夏日无踪夏乐游,一飘一荡一回头。
只缘巢旧心犹恋,袅袅余音几绕秋。

105

—

Do not insult your friend by lending him merits from your own pocket.

不要从自己的口袋里将优点掏出来借给朋友,那是侮辱他。

雕虫小技怎言高

别掏口袋觅功劳,借与良朋炫自豪。
侮辱换装几许巧,雕虫小技怎言高。

106

—

The touch of the nameless days clings to my heart like mosses round the old tree.

一接触到那些无名岁月,其触感就萦绕在我的心头,就像老树周身长满了青苔一样。

小触轻轻感纵横

无名岁月已无名,小触轻轻感纵横。
萦绕心头挥不去,青苔困树几悲声。

107

—

The echo mocks her origin to prove she is the original.

回声嘲弄着她的原点,以证明自己就是原创的。

郎朗回声爱自夸

朗朗回声爱自夸,讽嘲原点比其斜。
欲知怪诞缘何出,一手纯真二手差。

108

―

God is ashamed when the prosperous boasts of His special favour.

荣华富贵夸耀上帝对他特别恩典,上帝却感到难以为情。

苍天厌恶吹牛语

富户常常炫富豪,多亏上帝奖和褒。
苍天厌恶吹牛语,满面含羞兴不高。

109

I cast my own shadow upon my path, because I have a lamp that has not been lighted.

我将自己的影子投射到路上,因为我手里端了一盏从未点亮的灯。

一路匆忙一路登

一路匆忙一路登,自持阴影自持灯。
灯无火点灯无亮,路影吾身路影增。

110

Man goes into the noisy crowd to drown his own clamour of silence.

人走进喧嚣的群体中去,以淹没他自己寂静的吵嚷。

     杂音袅袅没山河

  嚷声沉寂待如何?喧闹尘寰闹更多。
  挤进人群消自我,杂音袅袅没山河。

111

That which ends in exhaustion is death, but the perfect ending is in the endless.

结束于精疲力竭就是死亡,而最佳之结束存在于无端点之中。

无限无端夜夜星

力竭精疲薄命停,兴衰胜败总归零。
欲知结束何为美?无限无端夜夜星。

112

The sun has his simple robe of light. The clouds are decked with gorgeousness.

太阳仅穿了一件朴素的光制的长袍,而云却打扮得花枝招展。

太阳朴素少浮夸

太阳朴素少浮夸,身着光袍晚送霞。
云彩多姿常打扮,胭脂抹罢又寻花。

113

The hills are like shouts of children who raise their arms, trying to catch stars.

孩子伸出胳膊,试图去摘星星,山就像这些孩子们在喊叫。

群山奔涌似孩童

群山奔涌似孩童,双臂高扬几闹喧。
若问缘何狂放浪,摸星揽月竞豪雄。

114

—

The road is lonely in its crowd for it is not loved.

道路生活于人群之中,却感到孤独,因为它不为其所爱。

孤独缘何几度闻

条条道路走人群,孤独缘何几度闻?
过往匆匆匆过往,可曾示爱半分文?

115

The power that boasts of its mischiefs is laughed at by the yellow leaves that fall, and clouds that pass by.

权势对其各种恶行夸夸其谈,却遭到飘落的黄叶和漂游的云朵的耻笑。

春花谢后夏花斜

恶资权势势资夸,黄叶浮云笑掉牙。
山水跟随风水转,春花谢后夏花斜。

116

The earth hums to me today in the sun, like a woman at her
 spinning, some ballad of the ancient time in a forgotten tongue.

就像一个女人在纺纱的时候一样,今天,大地在阳光下,用已经淡忘的语言,给我哼着古代的一支民谣。

大地微微向我歌

阳光今日特纯和,大地微微向我歌。
酷似纺纱前代女,民谣无序语言讹。

117

The grass-blade is worthy of the great world where it grows.

草叶无愧于拥有它赖以生长的伟大世界。

青青草叶遍寰球

青青草叶遍寰球,为谢隆恩美五洲。
个小身勤多贡献,寄生世界怎含羞。

118

一

Dream is a wife who must talk,
Sleep is a husband who silently suffers.

梦是妻子,必须喋喋不休;
睡是丈夫,得忍气吞声。

月朗星稀照九州

梦似贤妻喋不休,睡如夫婿闷声牛。

枕边王国无穷大,月朗星稀照九州。

119

—

The night kisses the fading day whispering to his ear, "I am death, your mother. I am to give you fresh birth."

夜晚亲吻着渐渐昏暗的白昼，在他耳旁窃窃私语道："我是死亡，是你的母亲。我将使你获得新生。"

黑夜温馨吻吻亲

昏昏落日渐沉沦，黑夜温馨吻吻亲。
窃窃耳旁安慰语，回生起死在清晨。

120

—

I feel thy beauty, dark night, like that of the loved woman when she has put out the lamp.

黑夜啊,我触摸到你的美了,就像一位被爱的女人将灯熄灭了的时候那样。

沉沉黑夜美无边

沉沉黑夜美无边,触摸方知秀比仙。
就爱吹灯神女暖,赏心岂在亮灯妍。

沉沉黑夜美无伦

沉沉黑夜美无伦,触摸方知秀可亲。
就爱吹灯人已醉,浑浑噩噩到清晨。

121

I carry in my world that flourishes the worlds that have failed.

我随身携带着我的世界,以便让那些已经衰败的世界繁荣起来。

我献些微富万村

衰败尘寰盼续存,上苍乏计活乾坤。
回生应有回生术,我献些微富万村。

122

—

Dear friend, I feel the silence of your great thoughts of many a deepening eventide on this beach when I listen to these waves.

亲爱的朋友,当我在海滩上倾听这些海浪的时候,我感到,随着多少个黄昏渐渐入夜,你的各种伟大的想法是那样的寂静。

临海观潮听浪声

临海观潮听浪声,君心寂寞夜渐盈。
腾飞思绪飞天际,我在沙滩感纵横。

123

The bird thinks it is an act of kindness to give the fish a lift in the air.

鸟认为，携带鱼到天空中去生活，将是一种善举。

群鱼若得翔天际

众鸟凌空自在飞，池中水族困幽微。
群鱼若得翔天际，大德隆恩胜日晖。

124

—

"In the moon thou sendest thy love letters to me," said the night to the sun.
"I leave my answers in tears upon the grass."

"在月光下,你把情书递给了我,"夜对太阳说。
"我则将热泪洒在草上予以回应。"

绿草传书胜雁行

黑夜柔情语太阳,情书赐我借蟾光。
感君不弃潸潸泪,绿草传书胜雁行。

125

The Great is a born child; when he dies he gives his great childhood to the world.

伟大天生是个稚子,他死的时候,将其童年留给了世界。

愿将无私铸爱村

伟大天生稚子魂,童年临死赠乾坤。
心如铁石俱含泪,愿将无私铸爱村。

126

—

Not hammer-strokes, but dance of the water sings the pebbles into perfection.

无须铁锤敲击,健舞的水唱着歌,便将鹅卵石带入了完美。

早随巨浪晚随涛

怎须锤击怎须刀,舞水欢歌善意豪。
卵石心高追完美,早随巨浪晚随涛。

127

Bees sip honey from flowers and hum their thanks when they leave.
The gaudy butterfly is sure that the flowers owe thanks to him.

蜜蜂从花中吸出甜蜜,走时则嘤嘤道谢。
花哨的蝴蝶肯定地认为,花应该感谢他。

蝴蝶承恩不思报

众蜂啜蜜返归程,临别回头谢几声。
蝴蝶承恩不思报,挟花缠朵要人情。

128

―

To be outspoken is easy when you do not wait to speak the complete truth.

做到直言不讳很容易,只要不等着把真话讲完就行了。

直言不讳有何难

直言不讳有何难,未毕真情句已安。
曲尽阑珊须忍耐,单刀破的爽丛坛。

129

—

Asks the Possible to the Impossible, "Where is your dwelling-place?"
"In the dreams of the impotent," comes the answer.

可能问不可能:"你住在什么地方?"
"住在无能为力的梦境中,"它回答说。

他日贤能问不能

他日贤能问不能,芳居欲觅几楼层。
难成一事存寒舍,梦境安家少永恒。

130

—

If you shut your door to all errors truth will be shut out.

如果把门关上,将所有的错误拒之门外,那么,真理也就关在门外了。

为防错误紧关门

为防错误紧关门,大失微差少地存。
此举灵通诚可庆,谁知真理遁无痕。

131

I hear some rustle of things behind my sadness of heart, —I cannot see them.

我听到,在我的悲伤的心灵的背后,有些东西沙沙作响,可我看不见它们。

颇难用眼寻

忧烦堵我心,酷似叶枯吟。
耳朵能听见,颇难用眼寻。

132

—

Leisure in its activity is work.
The stillness of the sea stirs in waves.

活动中的休闲是工作，
平静的海水在海浪中翻腾。

谁说休闲不上班

谁说休闲不上班，频繁活动活更艰。
远观海水平如镜，浪涌潮汐去复还。

133

—

The leaf becomes flower when it loves.
The flower becomes fruit when it worships.

叶子有了爱意,就变成了花;
花崇拜偶像,就变成了果。

循环往复了无涯

叶生爱意便成花,偶像花崇果实斜。
一物枯萎新一物,循环往复了无涯。

134

———

The roots below the earth claim no rewards for making the branches fruitful.

地下的根让水果缀满枝头却不要报酬。

根须扎地度春秋

根须扎地度春秋,愿助虬枝挂果稠。
辛苦年年从不怨,几曾思考索薪酬。

135

—

This rainy evening the wind is restless.
I look at the swaying branches and ponder over the greatness of all things.

这个下雨的黄昏,风一直没停。
我看着摇曳的树枝,思考着万物伟大之所在。

霏霏淫雨伴黄昏

霏霏淫雨伴黄昏,无息狂风扫百村。
目睹枝桠摇曳际,心思诸物伟何存。

136

―

Storm of midnight, like a giant child awakened in the untimely dark, has begun to play and shout.

午夜的暴雨,像一个巨婴,在不适宜的黑暗中醒来,开始又喊又闹。

悠然午夜雨倾盆

悠然午夜雨倾盆,漆黑违时醒巨孙。
耍戏多端多吵闹,一如大圣搅乾坤。

137

Thou raisest thy waves vainly to follow thy lover, O sea, thou lonely bride of the storm.

啊，大海。你掀起了海浪，徒劳地追逐你的爱人，你这孤独的风暴的新娘。

海婚风暴海心孤

海婚风暴海心孤，追爱掀波爱渐无。
睹此姻缘生恻隐，唏嘘掩面看通衢。

138

—

"I am ashamed of my emptiness," said the Word to the Work.
"I know how poor I am when I see you," said the Work to the Word.

"我为我的空虚感到羞愧,"词语对工作说。
"我一看到你就感到自己非常可怜,"工作对词语说。

硕果何年坠满枝

词语相逢实务时,内心空洞告他知。
繁花招展颇羞愧,硕果何年坠满枝?

困窘何时可展眉

务实闻言热泪垂,面临词语自生悲。
腹中贫瘠难倾诉,困窘何时可展眉?

139

Time is the wealth of change, but the clock in its parody makes it mere change and no wealth.

时间因善于变化而成了财富,可是钟在学舌中仅让时间变化,却没有让其获得财富。

多端变化富时间

多端变化富时间,学舌神钟热泪潸。
令彼无停终日转,何年换运换新颜?

140

一

Truth in her dress finds facts too tight.
In fiction she moves with ease.

真理一穿上衣服,就觉得事实太束缚她了。
而在非事实中,却能行动自如。

假地虚天任鸟飞

真理方穿事实衣,周身束缚一何稀。
换披小说诚宽大,假地虚天任鸟飞。

141

When I travelled to here and to there, I was tired of thee, O Road, but now when thou leadest me to everywhere I am wedded to thee in love.

啊，路啊，当我一会走到这儿一会儿走到那儿的时候，我疲倦了。现在你要带我到各处去转转，我却爱上你了，以身相许了。

与汝今朝坠爱河

独走东西旧径多，心生烦厌懒穿梭。
路为导引游天下，与汝今朝坠爱河。

142

一

Let me think that there is one among those stars that guides my life through the dark unknown.

让我设想一下,在群星之中,有那么一颗星,它能导引我的生活穿越黑乎乎的鲜为人知的地方。

夜幕沉沉黑幕垂

夜色沉沉黑幕垂,繁星闪闪耀天陲。
奔驰思绪生遐想,一曜牵吾渡未知。

143

Woman, with the grace of your fingers you touched my things and order came out like music.

夫人,你纤纤手指一触摸到我的物件,井井有条就像音乐一样弹奏出来了。

乐声袅袅绕梁旋

女人雅指涌音泉,撩拨吾心几弄弦。
万物井然皆有序,乐声袅袅绕梁旋。

144

—

One sad voice has its nest among the ruins of the years.
It sings to me in the night, —"I loved you."

有一种忧郁的声音,在岁月的废墟中筑巢。
它夜里对着我唱道:"我爱你。"

深深爱汝不心灰

凋残岁月废墟堆,忧郁情巢就势培。
夤夜悲歌夤夜唱,深深爱汝不心灰。

145

—

The flaming fire warns me off by its own glow.
Save me from the dying embers hidden under ashes.

燃烧着的火,用自己的闪光警告我快些离开。
免得我受到隐藏在灰烬中的将要熄灭的余火的伤害。

残灰炽烬暗藏悲

火焰喷光示远离,残灰炽烬暗藏悲。
千恩万谢难言表,救我平安脱险危。

146

一

I have my stars in the sky,
But oh for my little lamp unlit in my house.

我的星星在天空,
那是因为我屋里的那盏小灯,哦,没有点亮。

我撒群星亮九天

我撒群星亮九天,休疑此举出何缘。
油灯一盏存家室,无焰无光枕黑眠。

147

The dust of the dead words clings to thee.
Wash thy soul with silence.

那些死去的言语的灰烬总是缠着你。
用无言去洗涤你的灵魂。

陈词似土久缠绵

陈词似土久缠绵,阻碍灵魂上九天。
沉寂无声能涤垢,适时启用胜清泉。

148

—

Gaps are left in life through which comes the sad music of death.

生命中留有罅隙,从那儿可以奏出死亡的哀乐。

    几多罅隙铸人生

  几多罅隙铸人生,死鬼乘机害爱卿。
  一路悲哀哀奏乐,吹吹打打至埋坑。

149

The world has opened its heart of light in the morning.
Come out, my heart, with thy love to meet it.

清晨,世界敞开了他的光亮之心。
出来吧,我的心,用你的爱去迎接清晨吧!

天人合一历沧桑

清晨世界敞胸藏,快唤吾心浴早光。

大好时机休丢失,天人合一历沧桑。

150

My thoughts shimmer with these shimmering leaves and my heart sings with the touch of this sunlight; my life is glad to be floating with all things into the blue of space, into the dark of time.

我的思想随着闪闪发光的叶子而闪闪发光;我的心触摸到这缕阳光而歌唱;我的生命随着万物漂流进了空间的蔚蓝,时间的黝黑。

思绪追随落叶忙

思绪追随落叶忙,飘飘闪闪泛微光。
晨曦沐浴心欢唱,生活漂流乐意乡。
万物齐奔蓝宇宙,时间漆黑了无疆。

151

God's great power is in the gentle breeze, not in the storm.

上帝的权威存在于和风而不存在于暴雨之中。

寄宿和风款款飞

浩天赫赫最权威，寄宿和风款款飞。
暴雨逞狂施暴虐，上苍怎好托心扉。

152

—

This is a dream in which things are all loose and they oppress. I shall find them gathered in thee when I awake and shall be free.

这是一场梦,什么东西都松松垮垮的,它们都压迫着。当我醒来,我会发现他们都集中在你身上了,我也就自由了。

睡梦沉沉万物松

睡梦沉沉万物松,一何挤压一何凶。
自由之际吾将醒,聚集无遗在汝胸。

153

"Who is there to take up my duties?" asked the setting sun.
"I shall do what I can, my Master," said the earthen lamp.

落日问:"谁将在那儿替我尽责呢?"
"我将尽力而为,主人,"瓦灯说。

照料乾坤孰请缨

太阳快退问声声,照料乾坤孰请缨?
土制油灯忙作答,我将尽力到天明。

154

By plucking her petals you do not gather the beauty of the flower.

仅采撷花瓣,你采撷不到花的美丽。

惜玉怜香花瓣采

惜玉怜香花瓣采,篮装车载运回来。
问君美丽赢多少,颗粒无收几许哀。

155

—

Silence will carry your voice like the nest that holds the sleeping birds.

沉寂将承载你的声音,就像鸟巢承载着睡觉的鸟一样。

万别千差铸古今

沉默无声载汝音,一如睡鸟卧巢心。
谁言二者难相比,万别千差铸古今。

156

一

The Great walks with the Small without fear.
The Middling keeps aloof.

大与小结伴而行,毫无惧色,
居中则敬而远之。

居中苦索双全策

伟大闲庭伟小陪,毫无惧色几来回。
居中苦索双全策,边即边离扮介媒。

157

The night opens the flowers in secret and allows the day to get thanks.

夜晚秘密地让花开放了,却让白天去领受谢情。

夜色温柔百卉开

夜色温柔百卉开,人情辞却犯何来?
登台白昼浓妆毕,谢意全收怎不该?

158

—

Power takes as ingratitude the writhings of its victims.

权势认为,受害者痛不欲生是忘恩负义。

汹汹权势害人精

汹汹权势害人精,痛苦难熬不欲生。
霸主扬鞭连责斥,装模作样负恩情。

159

—

When we rejoice in our fulness, then we can part with our fruits with joy.

庆幸富有时,我们会乐意让他人分享我们的果实。

仓廪盈盈富有时

仓廪盈盈富有时,心存欢庆诉谁知。
兴高乐意分余果,携手人寰策马驰。

160

The raindrops kissed the earth and whispered, — "We are thy homesick children, mother, come back to thee from the heaven."

雨点亲吻着大地,轻声地说:"我们是想念您的孩子们,母亲,从天堂回到了您的身旁。"

轻声细语诉心扉

雨点如麻吻地霏,轻声细语诉心扉。
天庭羁旅常思念,今省萱堂一路飞。

161

The cobweb pretends to catch dewdrops and catches flies.

蜘蛛网假装逮露珠,却逮住了苍蝇。

设网蜘蛛捕美餐

设网蜘蛛捕美餐,申言露水好装盘。
苍蝇懵懂朝前闯,双翅齐拴小命残。

162

Love! When you come with the burning lamp of pain in your hand, I can see your face and know you as bliss.

爱!你手上端着一盏燃烧着的痛苦之灯走过来的时候,我看清了你的面庞,知道你就是幸福。

喜迎幸福几欢腾

相逢爱姊出楼层,痛苦燃燃手执灯。
我已看清君面目,喜迎幸福几欢腾。

163

"The learned say that your lights will one day be no more," said the firefly to the stars.
The stars made no answer.

萤火虫对星星说:"有学问的人都说,你的光亮有一天会熄灭的。"
星星则不置一词。

小虫萤火语繁星

小虫萤火语繁星,四射光芒不日停。
学者言辞诚可信,一词不置絮叨宁。

164

―

In the dusk of the evening the bird of some early dawn comes to the nest of my silence.

黄昏时分,那只某个清晨才出现的鸟来到了我沉默的鸟巢。

辞晨归鸟觅眠村

日渐黄昏日渐昏,辞晨归鸟觅眠村。
亲朋不见央求我,寂静为巢免掩门。

165

―

Thoughts pass in my mind like flocks of ducks in the sky.
I hear the voice of their wings.

思想从我的脑海里掠过,就像几群鸭子在天空飞翔。
我听到了翅膀扇动的声音。

一路豪情一路歌

脑海穿驰思绪多,颇如野鸭过天河。
凌空扇翅凌空越,一路豪情一路歌。

166

———

The canal loves to think that rivers exist solely to supply it with water.

运河总喜欢这样想,河流之所以存在,完全是为了给它供水。

新造宏沟设问多

新造宏沟设问多,自然何苦凿溪河。
现成答案无须想,供水人渠淌绿波。

167

The world has kissed my soul with its pain, asking for its return in songs.

世界用痛苦亲吻了我的心灵之后,希望以欢歌来报答。

红尘亲吻我心灵

红尘亲吻我心灵,不带温馨带苦馨。
安慰岂无安慰愿,高歌报答唱无停。

168

—

That which oppresses me, is it my soul trying to come out in the open, or the soul of the world knocking at my heart for its entrance?

压迫我的是什么呢？是我的灵魂想跑出来到露天里遨游，还是世界的灵魂敲打着我的心以寻门而入呢？

沉沉何物压身躯

沉沉何物压身躯，出窍心灵觅敞区？
世界神迷吾肺腑，敲门急急找通衢？

169

Thought feeds itself with its own words and grows.

思想以自己的词语充实自己,并丰富起来。

思想充盈谢语词

思想充盈谢语词,渐丰羽翼渐成诗。
小偈大颂知多少,长短高低尽适宜。

170

—

I have dipped the vessel of my heart into this silent hour; it has filled with love.

我将我的心脏之舟浸入了沉默的时刻,它便充满了爱。

吾心广袤颇能盛

吾心广袤颇能盛,浸入无声试重轻。
结果如何难意料,空腔已被爱充盈。

171

—

Either you have work or you have not.
When you have to say, "Let us do something," then begins mischief.

你或者有事干，或者无所事事。
当你不得不说"让我们找点事干吧"的时候，麻烦就开始了。

几多忙碌几多闲

几多忙碌几多闲，喝酒春游赏雪山。
一旦声言寻事做，麻烦种种扣门环。

172

—

The sunflower blushed to own the nameless flower as her kin.
The sun rose and smiled on it, saying, "Are you well, my darling?"

承认那朵无名花为亲戚,向日葵羞红了脸。
太阳出来了,笑着问她:"你没事吧,宝贝?"

葵花忍辱认无名

葵花忍辱认无名,满面羞红怒气生。
旭日抬头眉亦笑,问寒问暖问声声。

173

—

"Who drives me forward like fate?"
"The Myself striding on my back."

"是谁像命运那样催我前行呢?"
"自己大步流星地在我的背上行走。"

谁如命运逼吾行

谁如命运逼吾行,自我挥鞭趱路程。
三九严寒犹奋进,炎炎夏日秉星征。

174

—

The clouds fill the watercups of the river, hiding themselves in the distant hills.

云给河的水杯倒满了水,就躲到远方的山后去了。

河杯待灌请游云

河杯待灌请游云,库满湖盈暂惜分。
隐姓埋名山背后,再需续水再殷勤。

175

I spill water from my water jar as I walk on my way,
Very little remains for my home.

我一路走着,水罐里的水洒了一路,
到家时,已经所剩无几了。

出门取水踏归程

出门取水踏归程,一路淋淋一路行。
抬眼望家家不远,剩余怎够半锅羹?

176

—

The water in a vessel is sparkling; the water in the sea is dark.
The small truth has words that are clear; the great truth has great silence.

水装在容器里,闪闪发光,在海里却是黑的。
小的真理,溢于言表,清晰明了,大的真理却大音希声。

小理微词陈显义

水储缸桶闪星光,付与汪洋黑墨汤。
小理微词陈显义,恢宏义旨噤声藏。

177

―

Your smile was the flowers of your own fields, your talk was the rustle of your own mountain pines, but your heart was the woman that we all know.

你的微笑,曾是你花圃中的花朵,你的言谈曾是你自己山上的青松的簌簌声;你的心曾是我们都了解的女人。

几曾微笑似桃花

几曾微笑似桃花,万亩田园出自家。
侃侃高谈松木舞,群山奔涌响沙沙。
君心堪比贤良女,彼识吾知一朵霞。

178

It is the little things that I leave behind for my loved ones, — great things are for everyone.

我将那些小物件,都留给我心爱的人,大物件却留给每个人。

好施乐善救寒贫

临行小件未随身,留给家庭与至亲。
贵重大宗全赠送,好施乐善救寒贫。

179

Woman, thou hast encircled the world's heart with the depth of thy tears as the sea has the earth.

女人啊,你用你深情的泪水环绕着世界的心脏,就像大海环绕着大地一样。

女人眼泪淌溪河

女人眼泪淌溪河,缠绕寰球爱几多。
酷似汪洋环大地,同甘共苦两婆娑。

180

一

The sunshine greets me with a smile.
The rain, his sad sister, talks to my heart.

阳光带着微笑迎接我,
他的阴郁的妹妹雨点,三言两语,却滋润了我的心田。

雨点阳光骨肉情

雨点阳光骨肉情,仁兄晤面笑盈盈。
健谈小妹虽烦恼,润我心田岂盼晴?

181

My flower of the day dropped its petals forgotten.
In the evening it ripens into a golden fruit of memory.

白天，我那朵花，花瓣全都落，就被遗忘了。
夜晚，它成熟了，变成了一只金色的记忆之果。

弃美无人挂在心

白天花瓣落难寻，弃美无人挂在心。
夜幕沉沉催果熟，充盈记忆裹黄金。

182

―

I am like the road in the night listening to the footfalls of its memories in silence.

我像夜间的路,静听着各种记忆的脚步声。

几多阴雨几多晴

我如夜路少人行,静卧聆听脚步声。
往事纷纭浮脑海,几多阴雨几多晴。

183

—

The evening sky to me is like a window, and a lighted lamp, and a waiting behind it.

傍晚的天空,在我看来,颇像一个窗户,一盏点亮了的灯,和背后的一种等待。

等待潜藏身背后

夜空朗朗似天窗,一盏明灯耀大江。
等待潜藏身背后,驱云逐雾亮晨邦。

184

—

He who is too busy doing good finds no time to be good.

一心忙于做好事的人,却没有时间去成就自己。

碌碌忙忙务善行

碌碌忙忙务善行,手头未了又登程。
年年岁岁无闲空,岂有时间自玉成。

185

—

I am the autumn cloud, empty of rain, see my fulness in the field of ripened rice.

我是秋天的云,空空的,没有携带雨水,看着我的富足存在于黄澄澄的稻田中。

吾乃深秋一朵云

吾乃深秋一朵云,腹空寡雨荡殷殷。
金黄稻浪常翻滚,财富存储熟谷群。

186

—

They hated and killed and men praised them.
But God in shame hastens to hide its memory under the green grass.

他们仇恨,他们残杀,人们却颂扬他们。
上帝却感到羞惭,赶紧将自己的记忆藏于绿草之下。

几多仇恨杀苍生

几多仇恨杀苍生,偈颂纷纭未绝声。
上帝含羞难举笔,将其存入草蒿坪。

187

―

Toes are the fingers that have forsaken their past.

脚趾也是手指,只不过抛弃了自己的既往。

脚趾粗粗手指尖

脚趾粗粗手指尖,始分前后却无嫌。
自从那日人猿别,乃至尊卑这等严。

188

—

Darkness travels towards light, but blindness towards death.

黑暗在走向光明,盲目却在走向死亡。

      无睛有亮也难行

  沉沉黑夜向光明,盲目驱驰自丧生。
  追问缘由追到底,无睛有亮也难行。

189

The pet dog suspects the universe for scheming to take its place.

那只宠物狗疑心宇宙诡计多端,要图谋它的地位。

宠犬疑心几飙升

宠犬疑心几飙升,浩然宇宙好欺凌。
普天何处非王土,狗位垂危与日增。

190

―

Sit still, my heart, do not raise your dust.
Let the world find its way to you.

我的心啊,安分点吧,不要扬起灰尘。
让世界找到通向你的路径。

推门入室到前厅

吾心少躁且安宁,别把灰尘搅不停。
世界寻君知觅径,推门入室到前厅。

191

The bow whispers to the arrow before it speeds forth— "Your freedom is mine."

箭还没有射出去之前,弓悄悄地对他言道:"你自由了,我也就自由了。"

汝自由时我自由

未发之弓与箭谋,助君蓄势向冤仇。
离弦送尔嗖嗖出,汝自由时我自由。

192

―

Woman, in your laughter you have the music of the fountain of life.

女人啊,你的笑声里,鸣奏着生命喷泉的乐章。

女人心悦笑声喧

女人心悦笑声喧,生命喷泉奏乐园。
袅袅管弦飞袅袅,小河越过绕城垣。

193

A mind all logic is like a knife all blade.
It makes the hand bleed that uses it.

一个逻辑缜密的大脑就像一把面面锋利的刀，
一握到手里就鲜血直流。

且将逻辑比钢刀

且将逻辑比钢刀，长长短短各自操。
皆说多多增益善，双锋手握血滔滔。

194

God loves man's lamp-lights better than his own great stars.

上帝喜爱自己伟大的星星,更喜爱人间的灯火。

上帝非凡生慧眼

昊天星斗世间灯,轻重何须诉准绳。
上帝非凡生慧眼,红尘点点益怜矜。

195

This world is the world of wild storms kept tame with the music of beauty.

世界是狂暴的风雨,只不过其狂野被优美的音乐驯服了而已。

世界无垠暴雨多

世界无垠暴雨多,乐声美丽动情歌。
谁知狂野齐收敛,止息滂沱止折磨。

196

"My heart is like the golden casket of thy kiss," said the sunset cloud to the sun.

落日的余晖对太阳说:"我的心,被您一吻,便吻成了金匣。"

临别深深亲一吻

夕阳打烊欲回家,止步收身听晚霞。
临别深深亲一吻,吾心变匣嵌金花。

197

―

By touching you may kill, by keeping away you may possess.

触摸它,会有杀身之祸;离他远点,却会占有。

冷月蟾宫夜夜明

> 我我卿卿会丧生,远离久别益多情。
> 孰从孰去君敲定,冷月蟾宫夜夜明。

198

—

The cricket's chirp and the patter of rain come to me through the dark, like the rustle of dreams from my past youth.

蟋蟀叽叽叫,雨点淅沥下,穿过夜空,向我涌来,就像我年轻时候的梦发出的沙沙声。

蟋蟀叽叽叫不停

蟋蟀叽叽叫不停,敲窗点点雨遮星。
沉沉黑夜何时亮,既逝喳喳梦境腥。

199

"I have lost my dewdrop," cries the flower to the morning sky that has lost all its stars.

"我的露珠全没了,"那朵花朝着星星全没了的晨空喊叫着。

鲜花醒后语天穹

鲜花醒后语天穹,点点珍珠已遁空。
岂料九清宫亦冷,繁星正在逸逃中。

200

—

The burning log bursts in flame and cries, "—This is my flower, my death."

燃烧着的原木喷射出火焰喊道,"这就是我的花朵,我的死亡。"

火焰熊熊独木燃

火焰熊熊独木燃,声声呐喊震青天。
鲜花绽放层层艳,灰烬温温驾鹤仙。

201

—

The wasp thinks that the honey-hive of the neighbouring bees is too small.
His neighbours ask him to build one still smaller.

黄蜂认为,周边蜜蜂的蜜巢太小,
而他的邻居们却让他建一个更小的蜜巢。

黄蜂巢大自为功

黄蜂巢大自为功,嫌弃邻居宿小宫。
岂料答言惊四座,愿君弃大逐玲珑。

202

—

"I cannot keep your waves," says the bank to the river.
"Let me keep your footprints in my heart."

"我留不住你的波涛,"河堤对河说。
"让我将你的脚印藏在我的心底吧。"

愿将足迹寸心收

忽闻堤坝语河流,浪急波颠怎便留?
费尽玄机无妙计,愿将足迹寸心收。

203

The day, with the noise of this little earth, drowns the silence of all worlds.

白天带着这小小地球的嘈杂声,淹没了所有世界的寂静。

环球小小闹声浑

环球小小闹声浑,白日偕之走万村。
世界阴阳全串尽,喧嚣淹没一无存。

204

—

The song feels the infinite in the air, the picture in the earth, the poem in the air and the earth;
For its words have meaning that walks and music that soars.

那支歌在天空中，那幅画在地球上，那首诗在空中、地上感到无拘无束；
因为它的语言是有意义的，它的音乐在飘扬。

飞越乾坤诗有翅

浩瀚无垠卧太空，歌声并起越西东。
乾宽坤广均无限，如画江山季季同。
飞越乾坤诗有翅，意行音响四维通。

205

When the sun goes down to the West, the East of his morning stands before him in silence.

当太阳走到西方下山时,他早晨的东方已经悄悄地站在他的面前了。

东方拂晓亦难闲

落日西行欲下山,东方拂晓亦难闲。
悄声无语君前立,期待星辰巧换颜。

206

Let me not put myself wrongly to my world and set it against me.

别让我摆错了自己与我的世界的位置,让世界来反对我。

平生敬重地和天

平生敬重地和天,浩荡隆恩样样全。
世界同吾如错位,心孤影冷泪潸然。

207

Praise shames me, for I secretly beg for it.

表扬使我羞愧,因为我偷偷地乞求表扬。

阴差阳错各风流

恭维谀面面含羞,隐忍偷声暗自求。
百事千端皆有度,阴差阳错各风流。

208

—

Let my doing nothing when I have nothing to do become untroubled in its depth of peace like the evening in the seashore when the water is silent.

当我无所事事时,让我的一事无成在平静的深处不受干扰,就像海水寂静时海岸上的夜晚一样。

温柔夜色色柔声

手中无事事无成,休令烦愁乱意城。
海水深深深几许,温柔夜色色柔声。

209

Maiden, your simplicity, like the blueness of the lake, reveals your depth of truth.

少女呀,你的淳朴,就像湛蓝的湖水,表明你的真诚富有深度。

清纯少女一湖蓝

清纯少女一湖蓝,真意深深胜谷潭。
但愿天翁常照看,青春永驻似山岚。

210

一

The best does not come alone.
It comes with the company of the all.

最佳不会单行。
它由所有陪伴而至。

吾佳岂有子佳殊

人言最好永难孤,结伴而行历险衢。
你善何如他善甚,吾佳岂有子佳殊。

211

God's right hand is gentle, but terrible is his left hand.

上帝的右手温文尔雅,他的左手却令人生畏。

上帝如人手一双

上帝如人手一双,皆言左右两条江。
温文尔雅能资国,暴烈凶残可毁邦。

212

—

My evening came among the alien trees and spoke in a language which my morning stars did not know.

我的夜晚从陌生的树丛中走来了,操着一种我的晨星听不懂的语言。

虽然促膝不知音

夜神走出陌生林,欲与晨星叙古今。
可惜语言相阻隔,虽然促膝不知音。

213

Night's darkness is a bag that bursts with the gold of the dawn.

深沉的夜晚像一只口袋，黎明之金光在袋中喷薄欲出。

沉沉黑夜罩乾坤

沉沉黑夜罩乾坤，一袋晨曦夺袋喷。
蓄势金光寻势发，拨开浓雾亮千村。

214

———

Our desire lends the colours of the rainbow to the mere mists and vapours of life.

我们的欲望将彩虹的色彩赋予了生命的薄雾和水蒸气。

欲赋虹霞点雾红

雨后蓝天挂彩弓,五颜十色艳苍穹。
我之欲望生怜悯,欲赋虹霞点雾红。

215

God waits to win back his own flowers as gifts from man's hands.

上帝将花朵作为礼物送给人类，又等着从人类的手中收回。

鲜花朵朵赠凡尘

鲜花朵朵赠凡尘，上帝鹅毛厚意真。
俗子心潮随浪涌，万能懊悔与时新。

216

—

My sad thoughts tease me asking me their own names.

我的思绪在挑逗我,问我它们叫什么名字。

      倘若难知烦恼姓

    悠悠思绪乱心情,挑逗顽皮问几声。
    倘若难知烦恼姓,寻愁觅恨出无名。

217

—

The service of the fruit is precious, the service of the flower is sweet, but let my service be the service of the leaves in its shade of humble devotion.

水果以珍贵提供服务,花朵以香甜提供服务,那就让我像叶子那样,以谦卑地奉献阴凉提供服务吧。

我无特技几心伤

水果鲜花各献长,我无特技几心伤。
左思右想寻良策,如叶殷勤送荫凉。

218

一

My heart has spread its sails to the idle winds for the shadowy island of Anywhere.

我的心已经朝着闲散的风张开了风帆,以便航行到任何地方的阴凉的岛上去。

风闲浪散我心开

风闲浪散我心开,使舵张帆避暑灾。
欲问仙洲何处有,阴凉不必在蓬莱。

219

—

Men are cruel, but Man is kind.

人是凶残的,而人类是善良的。

大悟徐修心地阔

人为个体性凶残,物种灵群积善宽。
大悟徐修心地阔,急功近利速成难。

220

一

Make me thy cup and let my fulness be for thee and for thine.

把我做成你的杯子吧,让我为你、为你的人而丰满吧。

让我成君一只杯

让我成君一只杯,琼浆玉液抵沿堆。
子丰满赖余丰满,某打拼时汝夺魁。

221

The storm is like the cry of some god in pain whose love the earth refuses.

暴风雨像某个神在痛苦中大喊大叫,他的爱大地并不领情。

风狂雨暴几纵横

风狂雨暴几纵横,恰似神灵苦叫声。
欲问缘何凄惨境,无情大地拒真情。

222

—

The world does not leak because death is not a crack.

世界不会漏,因为死亡不是裂隙。

怎言世界漏流沙

怎言世界漏流沙？死损亡消树陨花。
生命循环非罅隙，不明大理乱弹琶。

223

Life has become richer by the love that has been lost.

因为付出了爱,生命才更加多姿多彩。

心存笃爱育新芽

多姿生命几飞霞,过往匆匆艳有加。
欲问缘何添异彩,心存笃爱育新芽。

224

―

My friend, your great heart shone with the sunrise of the East like the snowy summit of a lonely hill in the dawn.

朋友,你的伟大的心曾随着东方的太阳升起而光芒四射,就像一座白雪皑皑的孤山的山顶在晨曦中闪耀一样。

灿灿金辉灿灿光

君心逐日起东方,灿灿金辉灿灿光。
孤独山峦期拂晓,雪峰熠熠闪安详。

225

The fountain of death makes the still water of life play.

死亡之泉使得生命的止水灵动起来。

轮回更替轮回转

死似喷泉几助推，人生止水也葳蕤。
轮回更替轮回转，相反相成补益滋。

226

—

Those who have everything but thee, my God, laugh at those who have nothing but thyself.

上帝啊,那些富有万物而唯独没有您的人在笑话那些一无所有唯有上帝的人。

上帝资财两径庭

上帝资财两径庭,为蠋争辩问明星。
一方富甲微微笑,如洗贫寒读圣经。

227

The movement of life has its rest in its own music.

运动着的生命,在自己的乐曲中小憩。

生命长存运动中

生命长存运动中,乐含小憩奏融融。
张驰两济方成事,仙境人寰此理同。

228

―

Kicks only raise dust and not crops from the earth.

踢踢脚只能从地上扬起灰尘而不能收获庄稼。

应知踢脚起灰尘

应知踢脚起灰尘,怎让禾苗自现身。
劳作辛勤终有报,一年之计在于春。

229

Our names are the light that glows on the sea waves at night and then dies without leaving its signature.

我们的名字是光亮,夜晚在海上闪烁着,然后不签个字,就销声匿迹了。

姓名酷似大洋灯

姓名酷似大洋灯,逐浪随波黑夜升。
一字无留身已殒,销声匿迹了无凭。

230

一

Let him only see the thorns who has eyes to see the rose.

让只习惯于看玫瑰的人,不看别的,就去看那些刺吧。

玫瑰荆棘了无同

玫瑰荆棘了无同,扎手明眸互补中。
惯见鲜花开四野,更需斩刺走迷宫。

231

Set the bird's wings with gold and it will never again soar in the sky.

在鸟翅上拴上黄金,它就再也不会一鸣冲天了。

若用黄金饰鸟翅

万家求变万家寻,走兽嫌贫羡富禽。
若用黄金饰鸟翅,飞天不再怎高吟?

232

—

The same lotus of our clime blooms here in the alien water with the same sweetness, under another name.

同样是我们这个气候区的荷花,在这儿,在不一样的水里开的花,同样香甜,只不过名称不同罢了。

荷花气候两相同

荷花气候两相同,故地蓬生故地葱。
一旦池储他域水,花名异趣味仍衷。

233

In heart's perspective the distance looms large.

在心的视野里,距离便显现出来了。

距离长短有谁知

距离长短有谁知,境异时迁变换奇。
一旦丹心成视野,渐行渐远耐寻思。

234

—

The moon has her light all over the sky, her dark spots to herself.

月亮把光亮撒满天空,却将黑点留给自己。

　　　　　　　一把银辉闪朗空

欲知明月有何功,一把银辉闪朗空。
照亮红尘多少路,黑斑总在己园中。

235

―

Do not say, "It is morning," and dismiss it with a name of yesterday. See it for the first time as a new-born child that has no name.

不要说"这是早晨",就将它冠以昨天之名打发掉。要把它看成是还没有命名的初生儿。

劝君休再论清晨

劝君休再论清晨,昨日偕之别浊尘。
屡见犹如初次见,无名稚子履新人。

236

—

Smoke boasts to the sky, and Ashes to earth, that they are brothers to the fire.

烟对着天空、灰对着大地炫耀说,它们与火是亲兄弟。

手足情深命运同

袅袅轻烟炫半空,灰尘对地话豪雄。
二人转面恭维火,手足情深命运同。

237

The raindrop whispered to the jasmine, "Keep me in your heart for ever."
The jasmine sighed, "Alas," and dropped to the ground.

雨点悄悄地对茉莉花说:"请把我永远记挂在心。"
茉莉花"哎呀"一叹气,便掉到地上了。

大地开怀纳弃泉

雨点轻言茉莉边,请君将我记心田。
哎呀未竟珍珠落,大地开怀纳弃泉。

238

一

Timid thoughts, do not be afraid of me.
I am a poet.

怯懦的想法啊，不要害怕我。
我是个诗人。

夤夜清晨几琢磨

怯怯情浓想法多，羞于见我却缘何？
诗人总有推敲癖，夤夜清晨几琢磨。

239

—

The dim silence of my mind seems filled with crickets' chirp—
the grey twilight of sound.

我头脑里一片昏沉沉的寂静,却似乎充满了蟋蟀的叫声,那种天蒙蒙亮时的声音。

蟋蟀何来碧草鸣

昏昏大脑寂无声,蟋蟀何来碧草鸣?
微白东方天欲亮,渐行渐快响嘤嘤。

240

—

Rockets, your insult to the stars follows yourself back to the earth.

火箭啊,你那无视群星的轻蔑,又随你自己回到了地球。

唏嘘妒忌一时终

嗖嗖火箭入浩空,星斗含羞耻与同。
不料幡然回大地,唏嘘妒忌一时终。

241

Thou hast led me through my crowded travels of the day to my evening's loneliness. I wait for its meaning through the stillness of the night.

你已经带领我通过白天熙熙攘攘的旅程抵达了傍晚的孤独。我等待着穿过深夜的寂静来获得意义。

更深感悟夜琴弦

熙熙穿越艳阳天,来到黄昏寂寞前。
静气噤声持续等,更深感悟夜琴弦。

242

一

This life is the crossing of a sea, where we meet in the same narrow ship.
In death we reach the shore and go to our different worlds.

生命就是穿越大海,海上我们坐上了同一条狭窄的小舟。
死后,我们抵达了彼岸,走向了各自的世界。

命如苦海荡孤舟

命如苦海荡孤舟,船小人多怎应求。
死后须臾登彼岸,各家乐土各家修。

243

The stream of truth flows through its channels of mistakes.

真理的小溪流经那些错误的沟渠。

真理之溪缓缓流

真理之溪缓缓流,多渠错误荡悠悠。
众家水族争繁衍,尽在沿途浪里游。

244

—

My heart is homesick today for the one sweet hour across the sea of time.

我的心今天思乡了,跨过了时间的海洋,甜甜地度过了整整一小时。

吾心今日思家乡

吾心今日思家乡,穿越时间跨海洋。
六十分钟消失后,仍然沉溺蜜甜坊。

245

The bird-song is the echo of the morning light back from the earth.

鸟的歌声,是从大地弹回来的晨曦的回声。

众鸟缘何会唱歌

众鸟缘何会唱歌?晨曦射地返回梭。
随风起伏奏交响,吵恼悠闲好睡哥。

246

―

"Are you too proud to kiss me?" the morning light asks the buttercup.

晨曦问毛茛:"你骄傲得都不同我接吻了么?"

晨曦一出四方亲

晨曦一出四方亲,唯有毛茛独自珍。
旭日含羞连发问,缘何孤傲不伸唇?

247

"How may I sing to thee and worship, O Sun?" asked the little flower.
"By the simple silence of thy purity," answered the sun.

"我怎样才能向你歌唱、向你参拜呢,啊,太阳?"小花问道。
"用你朴实无华、寂静无声的清纯,"太阳答道。

清纯大礼慰平生

小花见日问声声,怎舞轻歌拜谒情?
朴实无华钟寂寞,清纯大礼慰平生。

248

——

Man is worse than an animal when he is an animal.

人为兽时比兽狠。

　　　　　　人为野兽时

　　人为野兽时，恶狠有谁知？
　　战火焚邻国，兄残弟杀之。

249

Dark clouds become heaven's flowers when kissed by light.

天上的乌云，被光一亲吻，就变成了花朵。

仙女撒花亮百川

朵朵乌云布满天，欲来风雨暗炊烟。
一声霹雳寒光闪，仙女撒花亮百川。

250

—

Let not the sword-blade mock its handle for being blunt.

不要让剑锋讥笑剑柄,说它钝。

参差互补股和肱

刚锋剑柄结良朋,锐钝纯因大异能。
有刃休讥无刃笨,参差互补股和肱。

251

The night's silence, like a deep lamp, is burning with the light of its milky way.

夜晚悄无声息,就像一盏深沉的灯,用自己银河的亮点燃着。

温柔夜色悄无声

温柔夜色悄无声,一盏孤灯伴五更。
深邃银河星斗众,供光送亮到天明。

252

一

Around the sunny island of Life swells day and night death's limitless song of the sea.

生命之岛阳光灿烂,而死亡却无休止地唱着大海之歌,起伏颠簸,夜以继日。

和煦阳光生命岛

和煦阳光生命岛,死亡浪海涌歌潮。
奔腾日夜何时息,窜跃升天跌地消。

253

Is not this mountain like a flower, with its petals of hills, drinking the sunlight?

难道这座山不像一朵花吗？小丘是它的花瓣，正在吮吸着太阳的光辉呢！

吮吸贪婪到日斜

远望山峦一朵花，丘丘似瓣染红霞。
阳光灿烂无穷尽，吮吸贪婪到日斜。

254

—

The real with its meaning read wrong and emphasis misplaced is the unreal.

真实的意义被错误地解读了,该强调的地方也强调错了,便变成了非真实了。

欲知真意费经年

欲知真意费经年,解读加强岂可偏。
对错混淆无小事,是非颠倒失山川。

255

Find your beauty, my heart, from the world's movement, like the boat that has the grace of the wind and the water.

一只小船拥有风和水，故而优雅，世界像小船一样。我的心呀，在世界的运动中发现你的美吧。

碧水微风雅兴娴

奉劝吾心逐美颜，红尘运动色斑斓。
一如荡桨驰舟楫，碧水微风雅兴娴。

256

The eyes are not proud of their sight but of their eyeglasses.

眼睛很骄傲,不是因为富有远见,而是因为戴上了眼镜。

双目洋洋得意时

双目洋洋得意时,诚非远见乐难支。
只因眼镜添姿彩,过往行人叹匪夷。

257

—

I live in this little world of mine and am afraid to make it the least less. Lift me into thy world and let me have the freedom gladly to lose my all.

我生活在自己的这个小世界里,害怕它有丝毫的减损。将我提升到你的世界里,让我自由自在地、兴高采烈地丢失我的一切吧。

自家小屋小柴扉

自家小屋小柴扉,吊胆提心损些微。
君界如能由我入,喜抛一切尽情飞。

258

The false can never grow into truth by growing in power.

虚假的力量虽然与日俱增,却永远变不成真实。

虚假虽然长势丰

虚假虽然长势丰,今生难与实情同。
渐行渐远长江水,只会从西淌到东。

259

My heart, with its lapping waves of song, longs to caress this green world of the sunny day.

我的心,以拍浪的歌声,渴望着去拥抱这个阳光明媚的绿色世界。

温馨一抱慰平生

我心拍浪起歌声,期盼红尘一缕情。
天气晴和原野绿,温馨一抱慰平生。

260

―

Wayside grass, love the star, then your dreams will come out in flowers.

道旁的草呀,去爱星星吧,那样,你的梦就会变成鲜花。

汝梦成花别样香

小草青青站路旁,缘何乏勇爱星光?
若蒙眷顾资生长,汝梦成花别样香。

261

Let your music, like a sword, pierce the noise of the market to its heart.

让你的音乐,像一把利剑,直刺市场噪音的心脏。

汝乐摇身成利剑

喧哗市场讨人嫌,昼夜不分闹意渐。
汝乐摇身成利剑,彼心直刺我心甜。

262

—

The trembling leaves of this tree touch my heart like the fingers of an infant child.

这棵树上颤抖的树叶,就像婴儿的手指一样,触动着我的心。

但愿秋风生恻隐

颤微树叶扣心帘,酷似婴儿手指尖。
但愿秋风生恻隐,缓吹寒气缓东渐。

263

The little flower lies in the dust. It sought the path of the butterfly.

那朵小花躺在尘埃中,她也曾追寻过蝴蝶的路。

蝴蝶当年几认亲

小花横卧在埃尘,蝴蝶当年几认亲。
逝路何曾寻觅少,去春过后盼今春。

264

一

I am in the world of the roads.
The night comes. Open thy gate, thou world of the home.

我在由纵横交错的道路组成的世界上。
夜晚降临了。开门吧,你这家庭的世界。

> 望汝开门迎旧客
>
> 我家世界路纵横,夜晚来临悄触楹。
> 望汝开门迎旧客,故园居室特温情。

265

I have sung the songs of thy day.
In the evening let me carry thy lamp through the stormy path.

我已经唱完了你白天的歌。
傍晚,让我掌灯穿过暴风雨之路吧。

风暴穿梭不畏难

白昼欢歌已唱完,黄昏渐至雨蹒跚。
君灯我掌通幽境,风暴穿梭不畏难。

266

一

I do not ask thee into the house.
Come into my infinite loneliness, my Lover.

我不想请你进屋。
我心爱的,请走进我永无休止的童年的孤独吧。

问侬怎忍独凭栏

无心请汝共厅寒,寂寞孤芳叹烛残。
幽禁蟾宫何日了,问侬怎忍独凭栏?

267

―

Death belongs to life as birth does.
The walk is in the raising of the foot as in the laying of it down.

死亡是生命,同样,出生也是生命。
脚着地时是走路,脚提起来时也是走路。

死亡亘古促新生

死亡亘古促新生,坠地登程向墓行。
酷似吾侪抬脚走,一前一后步方成。

268

———

I have learnt the simple meaning of thy whispers in flowers and sunshine—teach me to know thy words in pain and death.

花卉和阳光中有你的窃窃私语,我已经懂得了它们的朴素含义——请教我理解你在痛苦和死亡中的语言吧。

窃窃鲜花秘语传

窃窃鲜花秘语传,日晖达意拨琴弦。
个中底蕴吾皆会,痛苦登天义怎宣?

269

The night's flower was late when the morning kissed her, she shivered and sighed and dropped to the ground.

清晨亲吻她的时候,夜花却来晚了。她哆嗦着,叹息着,落到了地上。

低头诉与地球知

清晨准备吻花时,夜卉来迟误卯期。
太息声声言命苦,低头诉与地球知。

270

—

Through the sadness of all things I hear the crooning of the Eternal Mother.

透过万物的悲伤,我听到了永恒之母的低吟。

永恒之母浅吟时

万物忧伤我悉知,永恒之母浅吟时。
两相比较双张显,款唱低弹几许悲。

271

—

I came to your shore as a stranger, I lived in your house as a guest, I leave your door as a friend, my earth.

大地呀,来到你的岸边时,我是个陌生人;住进你的房子时,我是个客人;跨出你的门槛时,我是位友人。

我与寰球叙叙闲

我与寰球叙叙闲,呱呱坠地陌生颜。
敲门入驻家常客,离户成朋几日还?

272

—

Let my thoughts come to you, when I am gone, like the afterglow of sunset at the margin of starry silence.

我走的时候,让我的思想去见你,就像落日的余晖在寂静星空的边缘那样。

愿将思想赠明公

人去原知万事空,愿将思想赠明公。
宛如晚照微微闪,沉寂星边一缕红。

273

Light in my heart the evening star of rest and then let the night whisper to me of love.

请点亮我心头的休眠的晚星,然后让夜晚轻轻地向我诉爱。

晚星静静憩心中

晚星静静憩心中,盼你前来亮巨穹。
黑夜绵绵呈耳语,温馨起始爱无终。

274

一

I am a child in the dark.
I stretch my hands through the coverlet of night for thee. Mother.

我是黑暗中的孩子。
我把双手从夜幕中向您伸来,母亲。

　　　　　　　　　家慈搂抱暖东东

　　　我如夜晚一孩童,无辜潜藏黑幕中,
　　　面对萱堂伸手出,家慈搂抱暖东东。

275

———

The day of work is done. Hide my face in your arms, Mother. Let me dream.

白天的活已经干完了。母亲,让我把脸藏到您的怀里吧。
让我入梦吧。

天亮方知日耀嵩

白昼繁忙业已终,娘蒙儿面暖怀中。
温馨梦境温馨梦,天亮方知日耀嵩。

276

The lamp of meeting burns long; it goes out in a moment at the parting.

相聚之灯长明,在分别的那一刻才会熄灭。

善悟方能善始终

灯火长明相聚中,人离会散谢春红。
简单哲理人人懂,善悟方能善始终。

277

One word keep for me in thy silence, O World, when I am dead, "I have loved."

啊,世界。一句话与我存于你的寂寞之中。有一天我死了,我也曾爱过。

几曾恩爱意浓浓

弥留之际唤声侬,一句微言请记胸。
我本多情尘世客,几曾恩爱意浓浓。

278

—

We live in this world when we love it.

我们生活在世界上,我们爱这个世界。

红尘羁旅爱红尘

红尘羁旅爱红尘,缕缕情真意也真。
岁月艰难牵手度,春花谢罢咏秋晨。

279

Let the dead have the immortality of fame, but the living the immortality of love.

让亡灵永垂不朽,让生灵享爱不息。

重视情商重视情

但愿亡灵享美名,人生峡谷爱充盈。
看轻世俗看轻利,重视情商重视情。

280

一

I have seen thee as the half-awakened child sees his mother in the dusk of the dawn and then smiles and sleeps again.

我已经见到你了,就像一个似醒非醒的孩子见到母亲在淡淡的晨曦中那样,笑了笑,又睡着了。

嫣然一笑又蒙眬

看君酷似小孩童,似醒犹非睡梦中。
见母晨曦仍暗淡,嫣然一笑又蒙眬。

281

I shall die again and again to know that life is inexhaustible.

我将死了又死,从而懂得生命是没有尽头的。

红尘鬼蜮几来回

红尘鬼蜮几来回,欲探生机是否灰。
往复循环丝不断,以新易旧永徘徊。

282

—

While I was passing with the crowd in the road I saw thy smile from the balcony and I sang and forgot all noise.

当我同路上的人群一起走过的时候,看到你站在阳台上微笑,我便唱起来了,于是便忘了所有的喧嚣。

我放歌声吵闹终

熙攘人群大路中,与其过往走匆匆。
阳台站立君微笑,我放歌声吵闹终。

283

Love is life in its fulness like the cup with its wine.

爱就是充实的生命,就像盛满了酒的杯子一样。

人生有爱便充盈

人生有爱便充盈,酷似葡萄酒满觥。
大盏小杯交换敬,多情如许怎无情?

284

—

They light their own lamps and sing their own words in their temples.
But the birds sing thy name in thine own morning light, —for
thy name is joy.

他们点亮了自己的灯,在自己的神殿里用自己的语言欢歌。
那些鸟在您的晨曦中唱着您的名字,因为你的名字就是欢愉。

君名愉悦唤声腾

他们自点自家灯,外语欢歌越庙升。
众鸟晨曦呼子唱,君名愉悦唤声腾。

285

Lead me in the centre of thy silence to fill my heart with songs.

在你寂静的中心,请引领我用歌声充填我的内心世界吧。

茫茫广宇寂无声

茫茫广宇寂无声,我在中心独自耕。
诚谢先生多引领,余胸欢唱几充盈。

286

—

Let them live who choose in their own hissing world of fireworks.
My heart longs for thy stars, my God.

让那些自愿生活在自己的咝咝的焰火世界的人们去过他们的日子吧。
我的心期盼您的繁星,上帝。

星光闪耀我心驰

烟花世界响滋滋,谁愿安居自请之。
上帝听余明誓愿,星光闪耀我心驰。

287

Love's pain sang round my life like the unplumbed sea, and love's joy sang like birds in its flowering groves.

像幽深莫测的大海一样,爱的痛苦围绕着我的人生歌唱;像花丛中的鸟一样,爱的欢愉也歌唱着。

爱绕吾生诉苦情

爱绕吾生诉苦情,深如大海孰看清。
心欢似鸟殷勤唱,花艳花丛处处荣。

288

一

Put out the lamp when thou wishest.
I shall know thy darkness and shall love it.

你愿意的话,就将灯熄灭吧。
我将懂得你的黑暗,我将爱上它。

余情甚笃一何痴

熄灯与否自为之,黑黑沉沉我亦知。
手缩手伸难得见,余情甚笃一何痴。

289

When I stand before thee at the day's end thou shalt see my scars and know that I had my wounds and also my healing.

当我在白昼已尽的时候站在你的面前,你会见到我的伤疤,知道我受过伤,现在已经痊愈了。

西山日落立君前

西山日落立君前,见我疮疤未愈全。
伤损曾经常顾盼,就医岁月一天天。

290

—

Some day I shall sing to thee in the sunrise of some other world, "I have seen thee before in the light of the earth, in the love of man."

有一天,我会在某个别的世界里,在太阳升起的时候,对你歌唱:"我以前在地球的光照里,在人类的溺爱中见到过你。"

红尘坠入爱情川

他年我会唱君前,日出东方世界迁。
朗朗乾坤谋子面,红尘坠入爱情川。

291

—

Clouds come floating into my life from other days no longer to shed rain or usher storm but to give colour to my sunset sky.

云彩从既往的日子里飘进了我的生活,不再下雨了,不再为风暴导航,却为我的夕阳普照的天空添姿增彩。

万道霞光夕照红

云彩漂流我命中,痛抛旧习尚新风。
不漂雨点安狂暴,万道霞光夕照红。

292

Truth raises against itself the storm that scatters its seeds broadcast.

真理跟自己较劲,掀起了风暴,将真理的种子播撒到四面八方。

播种随风到广原

无常真理雨狂掀,播种随风到广原。
表面看来伤自己,乘机借力几翻番。

293

The storm of the last night has crowned this morning with golden peace.

昨夜的暴风雨,用金灿灿的平和为今晨加冕。

昨夜风狂雨暴侵

昨夜风狂雨暴侵,清晨旭日逐天阴。
冠霞覆地神州静,万物粼粼尽着金。

294

—

Truth seems to come with its final word; and the final word gives birth to its next.

真理似乎带来了结束语,而结束语却催生了后面的语言。

岁岁三春岁岁春

结语情长理已真,催生新意意更新。
层层推进层层进,岁岁三春岁岁春。

295

—

Blessed is he whose fame does not outshine his truth.

庆幸的是那种人,他的名没有让他的实黯然失色。

所幸乡邻颇认同

有人名望逐时红,所幸乡邻颇认同。
若使黄金镶败絮,有何颜面返江东。

296

Sweetness of thy name fills my heart when I forget mine—like thy morning sun when the mist is melted.

你的名字尽是些甜言蜜意,充斥着我的心,我却将自己的名字给忘了,就像雾气消散时的晨曦一样。

氤氲紫气退山林

芳名似蜜暖吾心,自忘身符各处寻。
酷似朝阳升起际,氤氲紫气退山林。

297

The silent night has the beauty of the mother and the clamorous day of the child.

默默无言的夜晚,有如母亲一样的美丽,又像孩子的喧闹的白天。

沉沉夜色美乾坤

沉沉夜色美乾坤,酷似娘亲亮丽魂。
白昼喧腾无止息,顽童小小闹山村。

298

—

The world loved man when he smiled. The world became afraid of him when he laughed.

人类微笑时,世界爱他;人类大笑时,世界却怕他。

微笑与狂笑

人生世界互依存,风雨同舟共一村。
微笑招来寰宇爱,狂欢吓掉地王魂。

299

God waits for man to regain his childhood in wisdom.

上帝等待着人类重新回到聪慧的童年。

耐心等彼返童真

当初人类特单纯,一路辛勤渐染尘。
上帝常年睁慧眼,耐心等彼返童真。

300

一

Let me feel this world as thy love taking form, then my love will help it.

当你的爱形成之际,让我来感受这个世界,那时,我的爱也会助它一臂之力。

一闻蜜熟情浓日

君爱成型我感之,人生历世探求时。
一闻蜜熟情浓日,愿助涓涓共写诗。

301

Thy sunshine smiles upon the winter days of my heart, never doubting of its spring flowers.

阳光将微笑铺洒在我心头的冬日上,对心头的春花,笃信不疑。

寒冬被我叠心头

寒冬被我叠心头,和煦阳光笑未休。
笃信冰融春不远,鲜花携手伴君游。

302

God kisses the finite in his love and man the infinite.

上帝抚爱地亲吻着有限,而人类却抚爱地亲吻着无限。

双唇吻出色缤缤

上帝心慈有限亲,双唇吻出色缤缤。
吾人大爱钟无限,微雨和风又一春。

303

—

Thou crossest desert lands of barren years to reach the moment of fulfilment.

你跨过了荒芜岁月的沙漠苦海,已抵达功成名就的时刻。

功成名就着鲜花

荒芜岁月漠眠沙,大地凄凉岂有涯。
汝历艰辛穿苦海,功成名就着鲜花。

304

—

God's silence ripens man's thoughts into speech.

上帝沉默无言,却让人类的思想成熟起来,变成了言语。

域外神州处处通

上帝无言立大功,促成人类思难穷。
一从想法连词句,域外神州处处通。

305

—

Thou wilt find, Eternal Traveller, marks of thy footsteps across my songs.

永恒的旅客,你会发现,你的脚印遍布了我的歌声。

一年四季岂能收

永恒旅客八方游,脚印如麻贯九州。
我放歌声君踏拍,一年四季岂能收。

306

—

Let me not shame thee, Father, who displayest thy glory in thy children.

父亲,我不会让你含羞。你让你的光彩展现在你的孩子们身上。

诸子荣光父有光

诸子荣光父有光,兴高采烈美名扬。
这般景象千人羡,我不羞亲万里香。

307

一

Cheerless is the day, the light under frowning clouds is like a punished child with traces of tears on its pale cheeks, and the cry of the wind is like the cry of a wounded world. But I know I am travelling to meet my Friend.

这天高兴不起来,阳光藏在颦额的云层里,像一个受到了惩罚、苍白的脸颊上还挂着泪花的孩子一样。风呼呼地叫,就像受伤的世界在哭喊。可我知道,我在去迎接朋友的途中。

今天兴奋一何难

今天兴奋一何难,颦额愁云日寡欢。
宛若男孩惩欠足,又如白脸泪犹残。
狂风呼喊惊三地,伤世呻吟恐九滩。
我有良朋需迎接,收心赶路正衣冠。

308

一

Tonight there is a stir among the palm leaves, a swell in the sea, Full Moon, like the heart throb of the world. From what unknown sky hast thou carried in thy silence the aching secret of love?

今夜,棕榈树叶有些动静,海在涨潮。圆圆的月亮,好像世界的心脏在悸动。你从什么未知的天空,悄悄地带来了爱的痛苦的秘密?

棕榈今夜叶嘻嘻

棕榈今夜叶嘻嘻,海水升高月似诗。
世界之心微悸动,爱情痛苦密难知。
何方未涉天空处,君带呻吟悄悄移。

309

I dream of a star, an island of light, where I shall be born and in the depth of its quickening leisure my life will ripen its works like the rice-field in the autumn sun.

我梦求一颗星,一个光的岛屿,我将在那儿出生,在加快步伐的休闲的深处,我的生命的杰作将会成熟,就像秋天阳光下的稻田一样。

梦境幽幽一颗星

梦境幽幽一颗星,光明小岛几娉婷。
我将生在林深处,信步如飞到敞亭。
作品成功名就日,金黄稻浪绘秋屏。

310

The smell of the wet earth in the rain rises like a great chant of praise from the voiceless multitude of the insignificant.

雨中,潮湿的土地散发出一股气道,就像从微不足道的无声的大众那儿唱出的伟大的赞歌一样。

雨中湿地起腥闻

雨中湿地起腥闻,酷似高歌赞美军。
有味无声声不息,衰微大众嚷纷纷。

311

That love can ever lose is a fact that we cannot accept as truth.

爱情随时都会失去,此说虽为事实,但不能视为真理。

常言情爱失随时

常言情爱失随时,几许真金几许诗。
起浪无风难足信,人寰定律亦非之。

312

—

We shall know some day that death can never rob us of that
 which our soul has gained, for her gains are one with herself.

我们知道,有一天我们会死去。但死亡不能剥夺我们灵魂的收益,因为灵魂的收益是灵魂的。

死亡难夺铸魂诗

大限临头自会知,死亡难夺铸魂诗。
得虽为得非常得,欲灭精神几许痴。

313

God comes to me in the dusk of my evening with the flowers from my past kept fresh in his basket.

在我的傍晚，上帝带着从我的过去中采撷的在他篮子里保存的鲜花朝我走来。

既往轻抛再铸魂

上帝看吾日已昏，鲜花在手慢敲门。
睹颜便识当年景，既往轻抛再铸魂。

314

一

When all the strings of my life will be tuned, my Master, then at every touch of thine will come out the music of love.

主啊,当我所有的生命琴弦被调好了的时候,你的每一次弹拨都会发出爱的音乐。

疾徐轻重情调节

我命成弦几十根,上苍弹拨触灵魂。
疾徐轻重情调节,钻石珍珠落玉盆。

315

Let me live truly, my Lord, so that death to me become true.

我的主啊,让我真实地活着吧。诚如此,死亡对我也就是真实的了。

大愿无多诉一声

大愿无多诉一声,上苍令我活真诚。
若能如此何其幸,畜死人亡各自行。

316

Man's history is waiting in patience for the triumph of the insulted man.

人类的历史正在耐心地等待被侮辱的人的胜利。

历史无公少水平

历史无公少水平,几多亏损几多盈。
宁心静气悠悠等,被侮翻身乐纵横。

317

—

I feel thy gaze upon my heart this moment like the sunny silence of the morning upon the lonely field whose harvest is over.

我感到,此刻你的目光凝视着我的心,就像清晨那阳光和煦的沉寂凝视着收割完毕后的孤独的田野一样。

吾心酷似一盆兰

吾心酷似一盆兰,敢劳先生注目看。
寂静晨曦天际照,丰收过后稻田单。

318

I long for the Island of Songs across this heaving Sea of Shouts.

我渴望,穿过颠簸起伏的呼啸之海,便到达了歌声之岛。

隔海欢歌绕岛旋

狂风呼啸巨波颠,隔海欢歌绕岛旋。
愿学仙人冲浪渡,借音起舞绿洲前。

319

The prelude of the night is commenced in the music of the sunset, in its solemn hymn to the ineffable dark.

在落日的乐声中,在献给难以言表的黑暗的庄严的赞美诗中,夜的序曲奏响了。

夕阳酷乐奏西山

夕阳酷乐奏西山,赞美诗歌唱几班。
黑暗沉沉难诉说,拉开序幕夜欢颜。

320

—

I have scaled the peak and found no shelter in fame's bleak and barren height. Lead me, my Guide, before the light fades, into the valley of quiet where life's harvest mellows into golden wisdom.

我攀登上了顶峰,发现那儿名声凄凉,高地荒芜,无处容身。导游,乘光亮还没有消失,请将我带进幽静的峡谷。那儿,生命的收获成熟了,就会变成金色的智慧。

步步艰难上顶峰

步步艰难上顶峰,凄凉满目少遮篷。
夕阳未淡良机赐,我愿神游峡谷中。
生命丰收安静地,可融聪慧铸金宫。

321

—

Things look phantastic in this dimness of the dusk—the spires whose bases are lost in the dark and tree tops like blots of ink. I shall wait for the morning and wake up to see thy city in the light.

在黄昏的昏暗中,万物均具幻象——尖顶下的建筑物在黑暗中消失了,树梢看上去像着墨的斑点。我将等待明晨醒来去观赏晨曦中的市容。

尘世黄昏万物奇

尘世黄昏万物奇,似真俱幻令人痴。
塔尖耸耸根基失,树顶斑斑墨点移,
但等明晨离梦境,曦微沐体市呈姿。

322

—

I have suffered and despaired and known death and I am glad that I am in this great world.

我遭过灾,绝过望,体会过死亡,令我高兴的是,我仍然活在这个伟大的世界上。

幸哉福寿仍绵长

失望困苦死难亡,大难无能把我伤。
尘世恢弘谁肯舍,幸哉福寿仍绵长。

323

There are tracts in my life that are bare and silent. They are the open spaces where my busy days had their light and air.

我一生中有过不少朴实无华、悄无声息的地带。它们都是敞开的空间,在那儿,我忙碌的白天享受着阳光和空气。

一生地域阔辽辽

一生地域阔辽辽,静默无华任画描。
敞露情怀忙碌碌,光浮气动赛琼瑶。

324

—

Release me from my unfulfilled past clinging to me from behind making death difficult.

过去,我留下了许多未竟之业,从身后纠缠着我,令我欲死不能。请把我释放出来吧。

反观往昔意难休

反观往昔意难休,未竟条条世上留。
日夜纠缠挥不去,无终怎敢入荒丘?

325

Let this be my last word, that I trust thy love.

让我用这句话来结束全篇:我笃信你的爱。

小集将成意气豪

小集将成意气豪,心潮逐浪浪潮高。
人言飞鸟难描绘,笃信君情汇爱涛。

飞鸟何时入我怀

——《绝句汉译〈飞鸟集〉》译后记

飞鸟入怀

飞鸟何时入我怀，今宵逐梦悉心猜。
人间多少糊涂事，月送花移自动来。

用绝句译完《飞鸟集》后，非常高兴，晚饭后散步时仍余兴未衰，于是便口占一绝。可回到宿舍时一想，这是新韵，不是平水韵。而我翻译《飞鸟集》没用过新韵，都用的是平水韵呀！于是便将上面的这首诗改为：

飞鸟入怀

飞鸟何时任我裁，今宵逐梦悉心猜。
人间多少糊涂事，月送花移自动来。

可后来又一想，这首诗有两个问题。第一，"裁鸟"这样的搭配，别人未必理解，如果将"任我裁"改为"慕我才"似乎又显得有

些孤傲;第二,这样一改之后,仍用《飞鸟入怀》为题就有些勉强了。于是,又将其改成了:

飞鸟入怀

飞鸟何时入我怀,今宵逐梦问钦差。
人间多少糊涂事,月送花移到汝斋。

这一首的长处是,将诗改成了对话式。可为什么要问钦差呢?这不明明是在凑韵吗?当然,这些问题解决起来并不难,请看:

飞鸟情缘

飞鸟何时入我家,今宵逐梦悉心查。
古来多少鸳鸯配,诚谢乔爷乱插花。

我举这个例子,不在于说明这首诗应该如何改,而旨在说明用绝句翻译《飞鸟集》会遇到许多诸如此类的问题。在这些问题面前,常常会感到江郎才尽,束手无策,尤其是在一口气翻译了八九首的时候,尤其是在原诗特别长或特别短的时候,尤其是在散体英译一连用了四五个仄声字或四五个平声字的时候。补充说明一下,为了方便读者的阅读与理解,我将原诗先用散体汉译了,然后再译成绝句。

一开始,总是想当然地认为,尤其在原文特别短的时候,五言恐怕是唯一出路。所以,前四五十首多半是用五言翻译的,七言用得很少。五言确有优势，短小精悍，如能注意选字，读起来颇有几分古色古香。当然这个优势我并没刻意发挥，因为在我看来，许多律诗绝句如《静夜思》之类，之所以脍炙人口、流传至今，一个主要原因可能在于语言朴实无华，容易上口，何况时至今日，如果用古词语写诗，吾恐和者益寡。

正如前面提到的，遇到散体译文中，接连出现几个仄声字或几个平声字的时候，尤其是在关键词避不开时，如"上帝"与"赠送"、"错误"与"正确"等，一时难以想到规避之策，很难遣词造句，只好诉诸古风，好在绝句有古绝和律绝之分。尽管如此，缓过气来之后，还是再写一首律绝，置于古绝之后，只有极少数在写完律绝之后，感到意义上离原文远了点，才补写一首古绝。

人世间，万事万物，优势和劣势总是伴生的。五言短小精悍，可字数太少，回旋余地有限，劣势非常明显，于是便尝试着使用七绝。别看七绝比五绝就多八个字，有了这八个字，想"做点手脚"就方便多了。请看：

　　一行一爱一姗姗

　　心潮涌浪浪侵滩，热泪题签几日干？
　　浓墨浓情浓笔底，一行一爱一姗姗。

这是第29首的译文。第一句"心潮涌浪浪侵滩"，不但重复了"浪"字，而且"浪"字承担了兼语角色，既是"涌"的宾语，又是

"侵"的主语。第二联可视为当句对,虽然"一行"等与"浓墨"等对得不够工整,但读起来依然音韵铿锵。又如:

缓缓熬煎缓缓诗

> 历史长流北斗移,吾侪显露恐难之。
> 匆匆搏杀匆匆客,缓缓熬煎缓缓诗。

这是第52首的译文。原文很短,主要是讲人生的,绝句汉译颇有些"添油加醋",然而我并不以此为憾,因为意义不悖本文,且第二联是当句对。不但是当句对,而且是反对(缓缓—匆匆),对得相当工整。

也许有人要问,为什么不以此为憾呢?我的回答可能颇具个性,但在古今中外诗歌翻译的文艺学派尤其在主张以诗译诗的人看来,译诗不是原诗的奴隶。在我看来,译诗虽然在形音义尤其在意义上,应尽量接近原文,然而却应该也必须自成体系。如按格律填词,或许不叫翻译,充其量只能称为"字译"。因为译过来的只是些支离破碎,远不是一件作品,更谈不上艺术品。

像第29首、第52首这样的译例在这本译作中还有一些。另外,也有这样的情况,用五言翻译了一遍之后,仍感到言犹未尽,又用七言再译一遍,如第51首、57首、58首、61首、65首、66首等,其中第65首中的五绝为古绝。

有时将一首原作译成两首,并不是因为技术上的需要或是受到

兴致的驱使,而是因为原文本身就有两个层次,例如:

世界缘何囿势权

世界缘何囿势权?豪言少礼藐苍天。
心雄助长乾坤欲,身陷牢笼叹惘然。

爱恋缘何享自由

爱恋缘何享自由?愿随世界度春秋。
乾坤四壁乾坤小,浪漫晨昏浪漫舟。

这是原诗第93首的译文。原诗本身分两个层次,旨在将"权势"和"爱恋"予以对比。但考虑到原诗虽然分为两个层次,却仍是一个系统,所以在后面又增加了一首:

权势·爱恋·世界

权势汹汹爱恋柔,面临世界比谋筹。
心骄气傲囚高阁,款语绵绵赐屋收。

第1首也与之类似。

别群

夏鸟出群飞,临窗沐日晖。
欢歌三两遍,小别几时归?

秋叶

秋叶已枯黄,欢歌早早忘。
随风几起伏,着地叹凄凉。

夏鸟与黄叶

离群夏鸟几临窗,欢唱声声告别腔。
秋叶无歌飘荡荡,长吁短叹落何邦?

略有不同的是,第93首的两个层次意义相反,互为对照,而这一首虽包含两层意义,然并无冲突。另外,前者为三首七言,后者为两首五言、一首七言。

一诗三译还有一处,即原诗第68首。原诗很短,为什么译成三首呢?因为开始动笔时,怎么也避不开"错误"和"失败"这四个仄声字,便将其译成了五言古绝。后来一想,可以将它们放到两个诗行中,于是又译了一首律绝。校对时又一想,七言回旋余地大,如果用七言翻译,就是放在同一诗行料也无妨,于是又译了一首。

还有这样的情况,原诗并无两个层次,但关键词有歧义,例如原诗的第6首:

If you shed tears when you miss the sun, you also miss the stars.

这里的miss有"想念"和"丢失"两个意思,且都可以引发tears。对此,一时想不到对应词,或者汉语就根本没有对应词,故将其散译为二了:

1)如果失去太阳就潸然泪下,你也会失去星星的。

2)如果想念太阳就潸然泪下,你也会想念星星的。

当然,也就对应地译成两首绝句了。因歧义一译为二,仅此一首,其余20首一译为二,都是由于其他原因。

现在可以总结一下了。泰戈尔的《飞鸟集》一共收录了325首散体诗,我手头的本子为326首,经查,第98首和第263首完全一样,故将后者删除了,还是325首。我将其译成了350首,其中一译三的3首,一译二的21首,译成五言古绝的6首,译成七言古绝的3首,译成五言律绝的61首,译成七言律绝的272首,译成六行的7首,译成律诗的1首。

为什么只有一首译成律诗了呢?为什么不将那七首六行扩充成律诗?道理很简单,律诗的颔联和颈联都要求对仗,有的甚至认为,如果不对仗,就不能称之为律诗。绝句不要求对仗,六行也没有对仗要求,虽然本集所收的绝句中,有一些对仗的例子。

我早就听说过泰戈尔,读过他人谈翻译泰戈尔《吉檀迦利》的文章,但一直没有读过泰戈尔的作品,直到有一天看到微信群里有人从《飞鸟集》中选了几首译成了七言诗。那几首译诗,句式整齐,押韵,平声仄声皆有,新韵旧韵齐备。读着读着,就萌发了用近体诗翻译《飞鸟集》的念头。

想法虽然有了，动手却很晚。主要原因是，课余时间主要用于创作近体诗、词和散曲，用于将自己的诗词曲译成英语。由于这个缘故，微信群里许多译诗项目或其他翻译活动很少参加，甚至不参加。尽管如此，读了译诗之后，《飞鸟集》对我的吸引力却挥之不去，于是便在网上搜寻，下载，动手汉译了。

现在回过头来看，《飞鸟集》中的诗对我来说基本上是一个全新的概念。第一，我头脑中的诗虽然不多，一般都是有题目的，即使没有题目，往往也标有"无题"二字；第二，我读过的诗，无论是汉诗还是英诗，甚至上中学时读的俄语诗，都是押韵的；第三，我读过的诗，包括部分莎士比亚戏剧，都有很强的节奏感。于是便倾向于认为，如果三者全无，是否还是诗？很明显，《飞鸟集》中的诗都是些无题诗，都是些无韵诗，虽不能说没有节奏，但至少可以说节奏不甚规整，接近普通语言的节奏。然而，它是诗，是地地道道的诗，而且早有人把它译介到国内了。

有人将宋词分为豪放与婉约两派。在我看来，我国的许多诗似乎也可以这样分。而《飞鸟集》中的诗，既没有"大江东去"那种豪放，也没有"杨柳岸，晓风残月"式的缠绵悱恻。读着读着，一个疑问油然升起：这是诗吗？难道仅凭人家说是诗，仅凭人家将其译介到国内，就认为它是诗吗？

回答这些问题，还是那句老话，"书读百遍，经义自见"。读着读着，我渐渐觉得，整个《飞鸟集》，到处都是意象，是一本地地道道的意象集；《飞鸟集》中的意象，往往彼此对别，相互交织；《飞鸟集》中的"芳草美人"不用于直抒胸臆,不用于表达缠绵悱恻,而用于暗示种种哲理,种种"道"。

例如,第1首中夏天的离群飞鸟、窗户、歌唱,秋天的落叶、无歌、叹息。两组意象组成了两幅美丽的画卷,相互连贯又彼此对别,汇集成了一幅大自然的季节更替图,暗示出大自然的"道"。

又如第3首使用了世界、巨大的面具、爱人、歌、吻、永恒等意象。世界戴上面具,是个庞然大物,取下面具,就变小了,变成了一首歌,变成了一次永恒的吻。怎么变呢? 条件是面对心爱的人。显然,这里的"世界",不是"大江东去"中的"大江",不用来表达豪情,也不用以表达缠绵悱恻,而是用于衬托爱的力量的。

再如第16首将世界拟人化了,将它看成了过客,赋予其行走、点头、离别等从我面前走过的动作,作者我则临窗而坐。显然,这个世界就是社会,而我所看到的,就是那些呱呱坠地和那些匆匆离去的人。

《飞鸟集》中的意象,不但有芳草美人、太阳月亮、大海高山等具象,有许多表示动作的意象,如吻、歌唱、叹息、运动、点头、告别等,还有许多抽象概念如正确、错误、真理、非真理、完美、不完美、可能、不可能、爱情、漆黑、明亮、寂静等,都拟人化了,都成了意象。例如第62首说,完美将自己打扮得漂漂亮亮的以赢得不完美的爱;第129首中,可能问不可能住在哪里;第155首中的silence(寂静),可以像鸟巢承载睡鸟一样承载你的声音,等等。

我没有将《飞鸟集》中的意象收集起来予以分类,但在翻译过程中,无论是散体汉译还是诗体汉译,都尽量保留意象。散体译文,一般能做到百分之百地保留,诗体译文由于受到句数和句长的限制,由于平仄和押韵的缘故,个别意象难以保留,个别意象稍有改造,如将"完美""不完美"译成了"完全""非完全"。在翻译很短的原诗时,有时会增加意象或者为已有的意象增添色彩。以第4首为例:

原文:It is the tears of the earth that keep her smiles in bloom.

散体汉译:是大地的泪花,使她的微笑变成了常开不谢的花。

诗体汉译:

大地轻垂泪

大地轻垂泪,群山尽着花。
红黄争俊俏,朗笑接天涯。

散体汉译中的意象,不多不少,一如原文,但"花"变成了"不谢的花",有所增益。绝句中则增加了"群山、红、黄、天涯"。然而在我看来,这些增加或增色,都是情理之中的。

正如前面所说的,开始动手翻译时,原文是从网上下载的,后来一位朋友给我发来了印度中央考古图书馆1955年印度版的影印本。特向有关网站、发送影印本给我的朋友表示衷心的感谢。

第一次将一本外国诗集翻译成绝句,不足之处甚至缺点错误恐在所难免,恳请方家和读者不吝赐教!

译者

2020年1月15日

When Did Those Stray Birds Fly into My Arms

——Postscript to *Stray Birds: A Chinese Translation of Cut Verses*

Stray Birds into My Arms

When did those stray birds fly into my arms?
I'll look into it in tonight's dream charms.
Many stupid things're done in world of ours,
And they will come with flowers in moon-shone hours.

Having completed the cut verse translation of *Stray Birds*, I felt quite happy and when I took an after-super walk, the happiness was not gone. Then I composed impromptu the above cut verse. When I reached my dorm, I thought in the verse, the new rhyme rather than pingshui rhyme is used. But in translating *Stray Birds* I had used the pingshui rhyme instead of the new rhyme. Then I changed the poem into:

Stray Birds into My Arms

When did *Stray Birds* like me to tailor them into Chinese?
Tonight, I will make a dare surmise when in dreamy peace.
How many stupid things are done wisely in th' world of ours,
And they come out of their own will with flowers in moon-shone hours.

Later, on second thoughts, I found two problems with the poem. First, the collocation "tailor *Stray Birds*" might not be necessarily acceptable to the reader. If it were changed into "admire my talents", it might seem to be a little aloof. Second, after the adaptation, the original title *Stray Birds into My Arms* might seem to be awkward in the new situation. Therefore, I changed the poem into the following:

Stray Birds into My Arms

Into my arms when did those stray birds fly?
Tonight, in dream I'll seek th' envoy's reply.
Many stupid things're done in th' world of ours,
And they will come with flowers to your honour's.

The advantage lies in the change of the poem into a dialogue. But why should the author ask the imperial envoy? Isn't it apparently for the rhyme sake only? Of course, it is not difficult to solve such a problem. Please see the following:

The Stray Birds' Luck

Into my home, when did the stray birds fly?
Tonight, to look into th' matter I'll try.
How many odd matches're made since time old?
Thanks to Lord Qiao for his arrangement bold.

I used this example not to clarify how to perfect the poem but to tell the reader that when the Chinese cut verse was used to translate *Stray Birds*, I had come across such problems all the way through. And in face of such problems, I was often at my wit's end and found no way out, especially when I had translated 8 or 9 originals on end, when the original was unusually long or short, when 4 or 5 oblique or even tone characters had been used in succession in the prosaic translation. By the way, for the convenience of the reader in his reading and understanding, I translated the original into a prosaic version before I put it into a cut verse.

At the beginning, I took it for granted that pentasyllabic cut verse might be the first choice, especially when the original was unusually short. Therefore, the first forty or fifty verses were mostly pentasyllabic, with only a few exceptions. The pentasyllabic verse is advantageous indeed for cramming compact ideas into short lines. If you are choosy in wording, your cut verse will read archaic. Of course, in the translation, I had not brought this advantage to full, for it seemed to me that the popularity of the most of the regulated or cut verses such as Li Bai's *In the Quiet Night* could be attributed to the simplicity of the language and the readability of the verse. In addition, at our time, if Classic Chinese were used in the translation, I'm afraid that it might not win much popularity.

As mentioned before, when in the prosaic Chinese version, a few oblique or even tone characters were used on end, especially when such a succession could not be avoided as shangdi (God) and zengsong (present to sb.), cuowu (wrong) and zhengque (right) and so on, I felt it hard for wording. At that time, I would turn to the verse of ancient style. Luckily, the cut verse can either be of ancient or modern style. Nevertheless, when I passed over the tension, I would write a cut verse of modern style and placed it after the ancient-styled counterpart. Only on very few occasions, after a cut verse of modern style, would I write an ancient-styled counterpart as a makeup if I found the translation a little bit too distant from the original.

In our world, for all things, advantages and disadvantages do exist side by side. Short as the line of the pentasyllabic verse is, it contains fewer words and has the apparent disadvantage of being confined to a compact space. Therefore, I tried my hand at heptasyllabic verse, which contains 8 words more. And with the extra 8 words, it will be convenient for me to do "some tricks". Now please look at the following:

One Walk, One Love, Slowly, Slowly They Go

Waves surge in mind and the beach they invade,
You write with hot tears, when to dry, my maid.
Thick ink, thick love, along the brush they flow,
One walk, one love, slowly, slowly, they go.

This is the translation of Original 29. In xinchao (tide of mind) yonglang(wave surges) lang(wave) qintan(invade beach), the word lang is repeated. In addition, it plays a double role, serving as the object of yong on the one hand and the logic subject of qin on the other. The second couplet can be regarded as an example of intra-sentential antithesis, although yixing (one walk), etc. and nongmo (thick ink), etc. are not regularly antithetic. However, the couplet reads phonologically harmonious. Another example is presented as follows:

We Suffer Slowly and Slowly Write Poems, Too

In the river of history, moving stars keep,
We find it difficult to show off for it's deep.
Struggle for good, as mortal passengers we do,
We suffer slowly and slowly write poems, too.

This is the translation of Original 52. The original is very short and it is about life. And it seems that the Chinese version has added much trimming to the original but I do not regret for the addition, for it has not betrayed the original and the second couplet of the Chinese verse is in the form of intra-sentential antithesis, and the words huanhuan (slowly, slowly) and congcong (hurriedly, hurriedly) are contrastive in meaning. And the whole antithesis is quite regular.

Perhaps, I will be asked why not regret for the addition. My answer might seem quite idiosyncratic in that I am convinced that it seems to poetry translators of artistic school, ancient or modern, foreign or domestic, that the translated poem is not a slave of the original. It seems to me that in terms of morphology, phonology and semantics, especially semantics, the translated poem should be closest possible to the original. However, the translation itself should be a system. If the translator only looks for verbal equivalents and fills them in the corresponding slots of the translation, then the product could at most be called a word-for-word translation. For what are translated are fragments, far from a product, not to speak of an art product.

In the present anthology, translations like those for Originals 29 and 52 are not uncommon. In addition, there are such cases in which the original is already translated into a pentasyllabic verse but I still feel it inadequate. Then I will translate it into a heptasyllabic one. The translations of Originals 51, 57, 58, 61, 65 and 66 are cases in point. And the pentasyllabic translation of Original 65 is of ancient style.

In the anthology, there is such a case that one original is translated into two not because the first translation is inadequate or my high spirits drive me to do so, but because the original contains two meanings. For example:

Why Should the World Restrict Power Its Free Rights

Why should the world restrict power its free rights?
It's bold in words, impolite, days and nights.
It has desire for the world large and great,
But trapped, it finds way out, useless and late.

Why Should Love Enjoy Freedom

Why should love be free to go left and right?
It lives with world for life, not out of wall.
With four walls around, the world is too small,
Love lives in boat of care from morn to night.

These are the two translations for Original 93. The original consists of two meanings, throwing "power" and "love" in contrast. Although the original is possibly divided into two, it is still a systematic entity. Taking this into account, I added a new poem as follows:

Power·Love·World

Power is turbulent while love is tender,
Faced with world, they'd know who's wise contender.
Power's trapped in an attic for being too proud,
Tender in words, love lives in house of cloud.

And Original 1 is translated in the similar manner.

Astray from the Flock

Out of their flock, the stray summer birds fly,
They stop at window in sunlight from sky.
They sing a few songs in praise of the day,
When to return, now they're flying away?

Autumn Leaves

Those autumn leaves are withered and yellow,
They've forgotten songs or even hello.
With the wind, they flow now up and now down,
With a sigh, they drop, not know to which town.

Summer Birds and Autumn Leaves

Stray birds stop time and again at window,
They sing good-byes merrily you might know.

With songs forgotten, autumn leaves flow down,
With a sigh, they know not down to which town.

The difference lies in that Original 93 contains two contrastive meanings while the two meanings Original 1 contains are not in contrast. In addition, Translations 93 are all heptasyllabic while Translations 1 consist of two pentasyllabic and one heptasyllabic verse.

Another example of translating one original into three is the translation of Original 68. Why should it be translated into three? The reason lies in that at the very beginning, I found that "cuowu" (wrong) and "shibai" (defeated) consist of four oblique tone characters. And it was difficult to set them apart in one line. Therefore, I translated it into an ancient styled pentasyllabic verse. On the second thought, I found that the two phrases could be placed in two different lines. Accordingly, I translated the original into a modern styled pentasyllabic verse. In revising the translations, I found if I should translate it into a heptasyllabic one, there would be more space for a line to accommodate the two phrases, and so I did.

And there is also such a case in which the key term is ambiguous. And Original 6 is a case in point.

The original: **If you shed tears when you miss the sun, you also miss the stars.**

where the word "miss" has two meanings. It means "to long for" on the one hand and "to fail to get" on the other. When it is used with "tears", the two interpretations are acceptable. Faced with the ambiguity, I failed to get an equivalent or there isn't an equivalent at all. Therefore, I translated the original into two accordingly:

1) If you shed tears when you lose the sun, you will also lose the stars;
2) If you shed tears when you long for the sun, you will also long for the stars.

Of course, I had translated the original into two cut verses accordingly. To disambiguate the original and translate it into two, the above-mentioned is the only case in point. All the other bi-translations (more than 20 in all) can be attributed to other reasons.

We can now summarize what I have done. Tagore's *Stray Birds* have included 325 poems. But the photo copy in my hand consists of 326 poems. I looked into the matter to find that Original 263 is identical with Original 98. Therefore, in my translation, I have deleted Original 263, hence 325 poems for *Stray Birds*.

Why was only 1 translated into a regulated verse? Why not expand the six-line translations into regulated verses? This is simply because in a regulated verse, hanlian (the chin or second couplet) and jinglian (the neck or third couplet) should be antithetic. Otherwise, the verse cannot be regarded as regulated, as commonly believed. For a cut verse or a six-line verse, antithesis is not compulsory. Nevertheless, in the present collection, there are antithetic couplets in cut verses.

I heard about Tagore years ago and read articles discussing the translation of Tagore's *Gitanjali*. However, I haven't read any of Tagore's works until one day I found in the WeChat that a person selected a few poems from *Stray Birds* and translated them into heptasyllabic Chinese poems, which are identical in line length, regular in sentence structure, rhymed but irregular in tone pattern and regardless of old or new rhyme. However, my repeated reading activated the germ of translating *Stray Birds* into Chinese regular verse.

Desire developed to translate it is one thing, repeated postponement is another. For I have to use what is left of the class teaching hours to compose Chinese regular verse, lyric poem (*ci*) and opera poem (*sanqu*) and translate them into English. Therefore, I seldom join WeChat translators in their translating activities. However, after reading the above-mentioned verse translations, I could not resist the temptation at the translation. Then I began to surf on the Internet, download *Stray Birds* and translate the poem into the

Chinese regular verse.

Now in retrospection, I find that to me, *Stray Birds* as a poem is completely odd. First, I have not crammed many poems into my mind's memory, but most of what I have kept are not without titles. Even if it is possible for us to come across one, it must be marked as *wuti* (the titleless); second, of all the poems I have read, either in Chinese or in English, or even in Russian as I read in high school, are rhymed; third, of what I have read, including some of Shakespeare's dramas, all bear apparent rhythmic patterns. With the bias in mind, I would ask: can a writing without these poetic features be regarded as poem? Apparently, *Stray Birds* finds no title for any of the poems. It finds no rhyme either. It can't be regarded as an anthology without rhythm, but all the poems are irregular in this aspect or it bears the rhythm closest to that of the ordinary language. However, *Stray Birds* is a collection of poems pure and simple, and it was introduced into China as such long time ago.

Song *ci* (lyric poems of the Song Dynasty) is usually divided into the bold and unrestricted and the subtle and graceful. It seems to me that such a division can be applied to many of Chinese poetic genres. However, in *Stray Birds*, there is no such bold and unrestricted line as "the Great Yangtze flows to the east", or such subtle and graceful description of "the willows on shore, the morning breeze and the remaining moon light in store". With this in mind, when I read *Stray Birds* repeatedly, a question arose naturally: is it a genre of poetry? Shall we make a decision on whether a writing is poem or not only by turning to the evidence that it seems to others that it is poem or that it was introduced into China as poem?

In answering such questions, I turned to the old saying: "Repeated readings can urge the essence of a book to come out willingly." I read it and read it, and gradually I found that every "bird" is an image and *Stray Birds* is an anthology of images pure and simple. It seems to me that of the images in the collection, each is different from another and all the images are interwoven. And the pretty grass and beautiful ladies in *Stray Birds* are not used straightly to express ambitions of the author's, nor are they used to express subtle and romantic sentiments but they serve as clues to philosophy or "Daoism".

For example, in Original 1, there are such images as flying stray birds, window and singing; and falling autumn leaves, songlessness, sigh. The two groups of images are knitted into two beautiful paintings, coherent but each different from the other, forming a picture of seasonal alternation and a clue to the "Daoism" of the nature.

Take Original 3 for another example. The poem uses such images as world, giant mask, lover, song, kiss and Eternal. When the world wears the mask, it appears as a giant. However, with mask taken off, it becomes small as a song or an eternal kiss. What triggers off the alteration? Face to face with the lover. Apparently, such a world is not the Great Yangtze in "the Great Yangtze flows to the east". It is not used to express bold and unrestricted feelings of the author, nor is it used to express subtle and romantic sentiments but to imply a force of love.

Take Original 16 for another example. In the poem, the world is personified into a passenger, endowed with such human acts as talking, nodding, departing and passing by "me", who sits by the window. Apparently, such a world is the human society. What "I" witness are human beings, including those who come to the world with a cry and those who pass away in a hurry.

In *Stray Birds*, images are varied, including such concrete images as pretty grass, beautiful ladies, the sun, the moon, the great sea, the high mountain. In addition, there are such action images as kiss, song, sigh, movement, nod, depart, etc. and there are such abstract images as right, wrong, truth, untruth, perfect, imperfect, possible, impossible, love, dark, bright, silence, etc. And all those non-concrete images are personified. For example, Original 62 says, "The Perfect decks itself in beauty for the love of the Imperfect"; in Original 129, the Possible asks the Impossible for the latter's dwelling place; in Original 155, "Silence will carry your voice like the nest that holds the sleeping birds." And there are other such examples.

I have not collected all the images in *Stray Birds* and classified them into categories. But in translating the original into prose or into verse, I tried my best to retain the original image. In translating it into prose, it was easy to retain all the original images. However, in translating it into verse, owing to the constraints imposed by number and length of the line, even or oblique tone, some images could not be retained; others might have to be reshaped. For example, wanmei (the Perfect) and bu wanwei (the Imperfect) were translated into something like wanquan (the Complete) and bu wanquan (the Incomplete). In translating a very short original into a cut verse, images might have been added to the original or a rich touch might have been added instead. The translation of Original 4 may serve as a case in point:

The original: **It is the tears of the earth that keep her smiles in bloom.**

The prosaic translation: It is the tears of the earth that turns her smile into ever-lasting flowers.

The verse translation:

When the Earth Lets Drop Gently a Few Tears

When the earth lets drop gently a few tears,

Mountains and hills're covered with flowers in cheers.
They strive to be richer, red or yellow,
To all corners the laughter will sure go.

In the prosaic translation, the original images are retained, numerically no more, no less. However, the original "flower" has been turned into the "ever-lasting flowers", richer than the original. In the verse translation, such images as "mountains and hills, red, yellow and horizon" are added. But it seems to me that the addition or enrichment is understandable.

As I mentioned previously, at the very beginning, I downloaded the original from the Internet but later a friend of mine sent me a photocopy of the 1995 Indian edition of *Stray Birds*. Therefore, I felt obliged to avail myself of the opportunity to extend my heartfelt thanks to the website from which I have downloaded the original and to my friend for the photocopy.

It is the first time for me to translate a foreign poem anthology into Chinese cut verse. I am sure that the translation is not short of shortcomings, defects or even mistakes. I earnestly hope that experts and readers will not feel reluctant to offer their advice!

The Translator
January 15, 2020